Keeper of Secrets

... Translations of an Incident

Keeper of Secrets
... Translations of an Incident

Anjuelle Floyd

Three Muses Press

an imprint of
Ink & Paper Group, LLC
Portland, Oregon

Keeper of Secrets ... Translations of an Incident
by Anjuelle Floyd

Published by *Three Muses Press*
an imprint of Ink & Paper Group, LLC
1825 SE 7th Avenue, Portland, OR 97214
www.threemusespress.com
www.inkandpapergroup.com

Cover design: Laura Dewing and Linda M. Meyer
Interior design: Linda M. Meyer
Editing: Laura B. G. Meehan and Linda M. Meyer

9 8 7 6 5 4 3 2 1

ISBN: 978-0-9769261-8-4

This book is set in
Palatino Linotype and Papyrus
Printed in the United States of America

*To Jon, for all the lifetimes in which he has loved me
and future ones where I will love him again*

Contents & Cast of Characters

Raven Clarke—a psychotherapist, and mother of three
Absylom Mugezi—a psychotherapist; Raven's former lover
Drew Clarke—Raven's husband, an attorney, originally
    Absylom's client
Alfreida Bryant—Raven's mother, a federal judge
Daddy Bill Bryant—Raven's father, and Alfreida's ex-husband

Lahni Ireté—a psychoanalyst
Nwoyé Ireté—Lahni's blind husband, a financier
Amos Morgan—Lahni and Nwoyé's friend; Lahni's
    colleague and rejected lover
Nicole Morgan—Amos's wife, an artist, once Nwoyé's love
    interest
Reynard Williams—Lahni's psychiatrist

Sahel Dennings—formerly a psychotherapist, now blind
    and on medical leave
Titus Dennings—a heart surgeon; Sahel's childhood friend
    and husband
Carl Pierson—a neurosurgeon; Sahel and Titus's childhood
    friend; Titus's rival
Reynard Williams—a psychologist (appears in Keeper of
    Secrets; The Object of Compassion); colleague of Sahel
Lillian Ohin—Sahel's mother

Reynard Williams—psychiatrist (Keeper of Secrets;
    As Far as I Can See...In a Day)
Aaron Blackwell—Reynard's wife and former patient
Ramona Bennett—Reynard's colleague; Titus's aunt/
    guardian (As Far as I Can See...In a Day)

The Bridge * page 101
Michael Banks—bridge engineer, recovering from a fall
Rachel Banks—Michael's wife
Greg—a divorce attorney; Michael and Rachel's friend
Carl Pierson—Michael's neurosurgeon (As Far as I Can
    See ... In a Day)

Three Movements * page 117
Ariane Gadsen—a psychotherapist who counsels the
    terminally ill and bereaved
Jack Gadsen—Ariane's husband
Gayle Clayton—Ariane's former patient, a lawyer who
    died of breast cancer
Raven Clarke—a psychotherapist, and Ariane's friend
    (Dancing Siva)
Renaldo Baptiste—a writer and widower

Myrandha * page 141
Trey Williamson—a successful architect
Myrandha—a model and Trey's wife, who died in the Twin
    Towers
Skip Williamson—the man Trey has known as father; a
    photographer
Anne—Trey's mother
Avron—Trey's uncle, a successful businessman

In Baghdad * page 159
Captain Daryl Sharpton—veteran of Desert Storm, the Gulf
    War, and Iraq
Lisa Sharpton—Daryl's wife
Chauncey Holmes—judge advocate general, and Daryl's
    friend
Drew Clarke—Chauncey's friend who lives in Oakland
    (Dancing Siva)
Raven Clarke—Drew's wife, and Lisa's new friend
    (Dancing Siva)

Dancing Siva

Raven stifled a yawn as she stared at the wooden icon of Siva. Another night had passed with her being awakened by the wails of her four-month-old daughter, Kaarin. Raven had gone to Kaarin's bed, taken her from the crib, and cradling the infant, lay down in the bed of the guest room. It had been this way nearly every night since Kaarin's birth. Kaarin never cried during the day.

Raven contemplated the mahogany carving of Siva dancing within the ring of fire. Its eyes, mere slits, appeared to widen. The icon's four arms seemed to reach out, beckoning her. Raven's soul was thirsty, parched from Kaarin's nightly screams.

Absylom's father had carved the statue now standing on the bookcase by Raven's bed.

Absylom had given it to her.

Two months after marrying Drew, Raven aborted Absylom's child. The fetus had been four months.

Now after sixteen years as Drew's wife, and mother to their three daughters, Raven stood searching Siva's face, wondering, as on every night when Kaarin cried, about the life she aborted.

Drew exited the bathroom while buttoning his shirt, and approached Raven. "It's last minute, but I'm meeting a client for dinner tonight. His wife is coming." Drew began arranging his tie. "I'd like you there."

"Why?" Raven turned from the bookcase.

"It'll make him feel safer."

"That's your job." Catching one last glimpse of the wooden deity, Raven began making her side of the bed. "Besides, my braids need to be redone. I don't know if I can get Nilini to sit." Raven resented the way Drew sought to make comfortable and defended the guilty. He inserted the second cuff link into the holes of his French cuffs, and walked to her, lifted her chin. "You look fine."

"My presence won't wipe out your client's sins."

"But it can help his wife."

"And, why should I help *her*?"

"Because I'm *your husband*." Drew let go of Raven's chin, then in the low, attorney-like tone used when addressing clients in public places, "We can't keep going like this. Kaarin's crying, this lack of sleep—it's making you cranky."

"I'm fine." Raven turned back to the bed and bolstered her pillow.

"You're not. How could you be? You haven't gotten a decent night's sleep since she was born."

Raven went around Drew and began straightening the covers on his side of the bed. "She'll be fine."

Drew followed her. "Let Kaarin sleep with us."

"She needs to learn to sleep in her bed."

"Like that's happening now? That's not what you said about Anisha or Emily. They slept with us for at least a year."

"Kaarin's different." Raven patted Drew's pillow.

"How is that? She looks just like you." Drew captured Raven's hand. She snatched it back, threw down his pillow.

As if knowing what lay hallowed and untouched between them for sixteen years, Drew slapped Raven with a stare of his own. His neck, the color of Georgia clay against his white collar, called to her. Raven searched Drew's brown eyes, inhaled the scent of his cologne, a mixture of eucalyptus and herbs. She imagined burying her lips in his neck above the mauve tie, and resting her head on his chest.

She sighed heavily. "I don't want to go with you tonight."

Raven wondered if her eyes were flickering green, as Drew said they did when she was angry. Absylom had said the same. She lowered her head.

"I miss you," Drew sighed. "I want you beside me at night." He leaned forward, kissed her forehead and caressed her shoulders. "The reservation's at eight."

Raven exhaled. Drew then whispered, "I'll be home at six-thirty to shower and change." He pulled away as he added, "if you care to come."

Raven had met Absylom her first semester in graduate school, as the two had stood waiting in line to register for fall classes. Taken by his accent, a mixture of Swahili and Hindi, she was captured by his plans to establish an ashram in the Thar Desert of Rajasthan, India.

"What's an ashram?" Raven had asked.

"A place for healing." Absylom's dark and penetrating eyes had glistened from within his mahogany face. He smiled. Raven's heart warmed.

"How will you help people heal?"

"I will use the skills my mother has given to me. I will teach them to meditate."

Raven was instantly taken. Absylom and his family had fled their native Uganda under Idi Amin's rule. He was educated in London, where his father, a member of the hearty Bakonjo tribe of the Ruwenzori Mountains, taught at a private school. Absylom's mother, born in Kinshasa, descended from Rajasthani stock of India.

Thirty-five and weary from traveling the globe, Absylom had applied to graduate school in San Francisco. He'd made a fortune as manager of a Hong Kong electronics company and wanted to take the necessary steps toward establishing the ashram in Rajasthan, India, that he had always dreamed about. Though Rajasthan was his mother's home, Absylom had never seen it.

❦ Life as the middle daughter of the first female African American judge in the Ninth Federal Circuit left little time for fun or reflection. Raven's decision not to apply to law school, but rather to pursue a master's degree in psychology had angered her mother.

Raven moved into Absylom's apartment the following month. There she began healing. Wooden masks carved by the Bakonjo hung on the pink-orange walls of their living room along with paintings of the Hindu deities—Siva, his white face held in a blue halo and his consort, Ma Kali, her teeth dripping with blood.

Raven's nightly meditations with Absylom after dinner, followed by their deeper quiet of lovemaking, eased her soul's longing for acceptance.

Using his mother's recipes, Absylom prepared meals brimming with curry and spices. Each night following dinner, he and Raven sat in front of the fireplace and meditated on the wooden statue of Siva, held in the shadow of the hearth. Raven's thoughts about her mother ceased when she meditated on the deity dancing in a ring of fire.

"Dancing Siva," Absylom referred to the icon his father had carved for his, Absylom's, mother.

"A god dancing?"

"Because he is angry," Absylom said. Raven searched Absylom's eyes as she had when they first met. A strange seriousness settled in. "Siva only dances when he's angry, like your eyes sparkle green when you are troubled."

Raven lowered her head.

"Do not be ashamed. Your eyes are beautiful."

Raven's eyes pained her. They were the source and evidence of who she was, and what divided her identity and loyalty to the man she loved as father.

"You will now meditate," Absylom directed.

"But—"

Absylom had kissed her. "I will join you." He placed his forefinger over her lips, and there, beside him, Raven envisioned herself floating in Siva's ring of fire, the deity dancing about her. Her mother's judgmental voice faded.

Raven lived with Absylom for three years.

At the outset of their fourth and final year in school, the man Raven loved as her father began to lose his battle against prostate cancer. Seniors in their last year of graduate school, Raven and Absylom had begun seeing clients at a counseling center in the Haight-Ashbury district of San Francisco. Each night Raven made trips across the bay to Alta Bates Hospital and sat with Daddy Bill. Meanwhile, Absylom, committed to building the ashram in Rajasthan, attended nightly speaking engagements to raise money.

Raven confronted him for not joining her at the hospital, "I need you there with me at night when I'm with Daddy Bill."

"I visit Bill in the mornings before I see my clients," Absylom defended.

"Perhaps if you speak with Theodore—"

"Don't bring Teddy Talbott into this!" Raven flushed.

"But Raven—"

She pushed him away. Her eyes flashed green.

The afternoon Raven learned that Bill Bryant had less than three months to live, she returned to the counseling center early. The student with whom she shared an office had yet to complete a session. Seated by the window in the reception area, Raven stared onto the street three stories below. She had not realized she was crying until Drew, having arrived at the center for his first session, offered his handkerchief. "Can I help?"

"My father has cancer. It's spread to his bones. He's the only one in the world I really trust. If I lose him—"

"But what of your mother?" He seemed determined to help Raven find hope.

"They divorced years ago." Raven banished the image and words of her mother, who three hours earlier had sat stoic and unfazed beside Raven when the oncologist delivered Bill's devastating prognosis. "I love Daddy Bill. He means everything to me."

Raven didn't speak about Absylom. Nor did she say she was a therapist training at the center.

Raven went into the ladies' room, wiped her face, and was on her way out when she caught sight of Absylom greeting Drew Clarke, welcoming him for his first visit.

One week later, Raven came to the counseling center early. Drew arrived and headed straight to where she again sat by the window. She had been waiting.

"How are you doing?" He sat next to her.

"Fine." She tilted her face toward the window and forced a smile.

"How could that be? Your father's dying, you're not fine."

The fear and sadness she kept at bay when with Absylom flooded forth. She flushed. Drew said, "When my session's over, I'd like to take you to dinner—that is, if you'd care to eat with me."

Raven's lips trembled. "I'd like that. But I won't be free until six." She said nothing of her relationship with Absylom.

"I'll pick you up at six," Drew said. It was then almost three.

"How about six thirty? I'll meet you at the corner across from the coffee shop." She pointed out the window. Absylom was scheduled to see clients until late that evening—nine o'clock—after which he was meeting a fellow student interested in donating time at the ashram once it was built.

Drew pulled his attention from the street below. "I'm looking forward to it." Raven smiled, then excused herself to the bathroom. She didn't want to chance Absylom seeing her when he came out to greet Drew.

While in the ladies' room, she berated herself for lying to Drew. But his comforting voice and self-assurance gave her hope that she could survive the coming days of Bill slipping away, and his eventual absence.

Raven saw her last client, then hurried down from the

counseling center to the corner across from the coffee shop. Not knowing what kind of car Drew drove, she peered into all the parked ones. They were all empty.

"Hi. You came early." Raven turned back toward the familiar voice. "I arrived an hour ago, came in here to have tea," Drew escorted her inside the coffee shop. "Our reservations aren't until eight. Would you like something?" He pulled out her chair.

"Coffee." Raven compelled her lips to remain calm, as she sat. Absylom liked tea and was known to stroll down to the coffee shop between clients when he was working late.

Drew returned with Raven's coffee. Over carefully neutral conversation, she sipped her coffee, and Drew his tea. Absylom made no appearance.

Raven ate dinner with Drew at a restaurant in the North End. Across town and away from the coffee shop near the counseling center, Raven became more relaxed. The meal was light, chicken piccata in lemon sauce and herbs with spinach. Drew had mussels and clams with pasta and marinara sauce.

"So how long have you been coming to the counseling center?" Drew asked while winding some angel-hair pasta onto his fork.

Wiping her mouth, Raven let the napkin linger over her lips, then said, "Oh for about a year." She and Absylom had been training at the center for nine months.

"Whom do you see—which therapist are you working with?"

"A woman." Raven placed her napkin on the table beside her plate.

"I'm sorry. I didn't mean to pry. I'm seeing this guy named Absylom Mugezi." Drew lowered his fork onto his plate. "I've never done this—seen a therapist, that is." He turned away.

"No. It's okay." Raven reached across the table and touched his hand. "You're concerned. I like that." Again she felt horrible for lying, leading him to believe she was a client. "Is your therapist helping you?"

"Yeah. I like him." Drew's brown eyes again softened with concern. "You seemed so lost the day I walked in. Do you talk about these things with your therapist?" It was as if, despite what she'd said, Drew considered Absylom to be Raven's therapist—that on some level Drew knew that Raven felt abandoned by Absylom as her father was dying.

"She listens," Raven said. "It's just that no one's prepared for death."

"Our own—or someone else's?" Drew queried.

"No one is. Ever." Raven said.

"I was prepared for my father's death. When I was a child." Drew's lips were straight. "My father served two tours of duty in Vietnam."

Raven sensed venom and hurt flowing underneath Drew's words.

He finished his dinner, silence binding them as she watched and wondered about the nature of this man whose care so calmed her and to whom she was growing more attracted.

Afterward, Drew drove her across the bridge to the hospital in Berkeley.

That night, as they did time and again, Raven sat beside Daddy Bill's hospital bed, Drew next to her. She held Bill's hand as he slept, and Drew held Raven's while she prayed that she would survive Bill's death and find the strength to tell Drew that she was not a client, but a therapist, more specifically, the one who lived and slept with his therapist, Absylom Mugezi.

Raven continued to meet Drew on Wednesdays after she finished at the center. She ate dinner with him, after which he drove her to see Bill at the hospital in Berkeley. One evening while sitting beside Bill's bed, watching him sleep, Raven said of Bill, "He was a good man," then confided, "Momma was so mean to him."

Drew squeezed Raven's hand tightly. "Sometimes our parents do things they don't mean, things neither we nor they understand. They just want the best for us." Drew looked down. "My father was hard-nosed during my childhood. I hated him." An army colonel, Drew's father was an orthopedic surgeon near the 38th Parallel.

"Is that why you're seeing Absylom? I mean Mr. Mugezi," Raven corrected.

Drew's eyes became alert. Perhaps it was the way she had said the name, Absylom, the lilt in her voice, or just that she had retracted to the formal.

Drew's face, brown with red undertones, relaxed. "Absylom won't have any of that—me calling him Mr. Mugezi. That's why I like talking to him." Drew again glanced at the floor. "I've got a lot of anger toward him— my dad. I love him—my dad, but—"

Raven sucked in air. Drew embraced her, pulled her head onto his chest, and brushed her cheek. For the first time in a long while, Raven felt safe.

As Bill grew weaker over the next two months Raven's Wednesday night routine with Drew extended to other nights, and throughout the week. Drew became her bulwark. At times, on awakening, Bill talked with Drew. The two of them had an easy way with each other, less formal than when Bill spoke with Absylom, whom Bill, not unlike Raven, always saw as a teacher.

Eager to maintain support for the ashram he planned to build, Absylom rarely came home before midnight. Raven often arrived home minutes before Absylom, relieving her from having to explain her whereabouts except to say on those occasions when she did, that she had either been to the library or was walking to clear her head after a session with a client.

A week before Bill's death, Raven met Drew at the corner across from the coffee shop. He was standing by his car.

"Can we go inside for a moment? I need a bit of tea." Raven

had noticed during their dinners that Drew liked sipping tea after what he described as an exceptionally grueling day at work, or when having left late from his office as in-house counsel for a Silicon Valley company, he had braved thick traffic from the peninsula to San Francisco.

Inside the coffee shop, Drew ordered her usual coffee and his cup of tea. After setting their cups on the table, he slumped down in his chair across from her. "Thanks," he said. "I just needed a moment to gather myself." Drew's eyes retreated. He seemed confused, disturbed. "For a moment I forgot where our reservations were."

"Don't worry. We can grab something over in Berkeley," Raven said, concerned. "In fact let me drive." Drew lived in Palo Alto. "I'll bring you back here to your car, then drive myself home." Drew usually drove them over to Berkeley and then took her back to school, from where she walked home. It was a great cover in case Absylom wondered where she had been.

"No. That's okay. I called my secretary and she told me where she'd made the reservations ... I need to talk." Raven grew tense. Two months had passed since she met Drew, and Bill was near death. She had promised herself and Bill that she would tell Drew the truth about her relationship with Absylom. And now he needed her.

"I had a difficult session with Mugezi today." Drew ran his forefinger along the rim of his cup.

Suppressing her fears, she quietly asked, "What did you talk about?"

"My father, as always." Drew regarded her from across the table. "And my mother." Raven released her breath and, without realizing, assumed her listening mode for clients.

"My father had changed when he came home that second time from Vietnam. He didn't drink—just poured the scotch and stared at it. Afterward he'd put the glass in the sink. Nothing would be gone, if only a drop." Drew placed both hands on his cup. "One night when he set the glass in the sink, Mom was on a stepladder. He turned around. He was sullen like always after holding the glass."

Raven grew anxious to hear the outcome of Drew's story. She cared about his well-being, cared about *him*.

"I don't know what happened. But my mother fell—"

"Raven." She whipped around, and took in Absylom's smooth, dark face. His dolorous eyes slid from her to Drew, who was shaken by the interruption. "How are you feeling?" Absylom asked, with tea in hand.

"Today's session was a little rough." Drew sat up straight.

"He was just sharing it with me." Raven forced the words.

Absylom smiled, apparently reassured that Raven was with Drew, then said to him, "It seems you found someone to talk to."

She knew Absylom would not divulge his relationship with Drew. *How absurd,* she thought. *He doesn't know. Neither of them know.*

"I'll leave you alone," Absylom said. "Call me if you need to." He left.

Drew relaxed his shoulders. "That was my therapist."

"I know."

Again Drew searched Raven's eyes.

"I mean, I've seen him around the center, when I've been waiting to see my therapist." Raven tried covering her tracks. "He seems nice, like he really cares." Drew continued to inspect her eyes as when she had said Absylom's name, and while Drew had spoke of anticipating his father's death in Vietnam, and of Drew making a decision to seek counseling.

"I'm hungry." He tore his eyes from Raven's and stood. "And you need to eat." They left with Drew acquiescing to her offer to drive and also that they skip dinner in the City.

Over Korean food at a little place near the hospital in Berkeley, unspoken questions cast a pall over their meal. The awkward silence persisted as they later sat at Bill's bedside.

An hour passed with Raven keeping vigil beside Bill, his hand sandwiched between her palms. She had not reached for Drew's hand, nor had he offered it. On seeing that her father was not about to wake—the nurse had given him a dose of morphine—Raven silently gathered her purse to leave.

They had just cleared the doorway and entered the corridor when Raven turned to Drew and said, "I know your therapist."

"Is Mugezi your therapist too? I know you said you were seeing a woman, but—"

"No," Raven said. Drew's eyes seemed to search for links explaining what Raven had sensed Drew witnessed flowing between her and Absylom when he encountered her and Drew in the coffee shop.

"We're in school together," Raven said. Drew's energy faded. She added, "I've lived with him the past three years."

He grew still, his eyes silent yet sharp, as if he had been hit with unexpected information while in court.

"I'm not a client," Raven said. "I'm in my last year of study for my master's in psychology. Abyslom and I are seeing clients as required for graduation."

Again Drew studied her eyes. He pushed his hands into his pockets, and walked away.

"How will you get home?" Raven rushed after him. Drew kept walking. "Let me at least—"

The elevator doors parted, and he stepped on. They closed. Raven felt hope diminishing like a treasured sailboat released onto the water and drifting away.

Raven returned to Bill's hospital room and watched the nurse plump the pillow underneath Bill's head before heading for the parking lot and San Francisco.

On the approach to the Bay Bridge, Raven called Alfreida and explained her dilemma. "I'm worried about him," she said of Drew.

"As well you should be." A judge, Alfreida was good at dispensing judgment. "Drew Clarke is not the sort of man to put up with Absylom's leftovers."

"I'm not ashamed of my time with Absylom."

"If that were the case, then why did you wait so long to tell Drew the truth?"

"I didn't want to hurt him."

"It seems you've done just that."

Raven had found in Absylom a well of compassion. She had learned much from him. And then Daddy Bill grew sick with cancer. Drew gave Raven constancy, safety. She wanted to share, live out with Drew what she had learned from Absylom.

"Momma, I'm calling you for help."

"And I'm giving it."

"No you're not. You're just judging me as always." Alfreida had been furious at her for moving in with Abyslom. Raven resented the fact that she didn't have a therapist with whom to discuss these issues.

She had started seeing someone at the outset of entering graduate school, but attempting to discuss her frustrations toward Alfreida became more than Raven could tolerate. Remaining with Abyslom, meditating with him each night, became her form of escape from her and Alfreida's own conflicting brew of emotions that bound them together.

Alfreida's words resounded through the cell phone and sliced through Raven. "You need to call Drew and apologize. Tell him that you made a terrible mistake moving in with Absylom." Drew respected Absylom, something that Alfreida refused to acknowledge. "That's what you say, Raven. And I beg to differ. With you in his life, Drew would have no need for Absylom." Raven also knew that taking Drew into her life would rid Alfreida's life of Absylom.

"I love Drew, Momma. But Absylom has taught me a lot."

"And you know where I stand." Alfreida had met Drew when Raven had invited him over for dinner. As always,

Teddy Talbott, Alfreida's longtime confidante, had been present. Alfreida liked Drew and all he represented, and Teddy was glad to see Alfreida smiling, particularly at something Raven had done.

Alfreida said, "No woman's life is big enough for two men, unless she wants to end up dead, either by their hand or by killing herself in an attempt to love them both."

Raven clicked off the phone.

On arriving back at the apartment in the city, Raven went directly to bed. She was asleep when Absylom arrived later and slipped into bed beside her. She awoke early the next morning, went to class and then to the counseling center. She would tell him about Drew that evening.

.ᘓᔭ.

Seconds before her first client was due, the telephone rang. Raven placed the receiver to her ear. Alfreida's voice announced, "Bill just died."

❧ Raven entered the apartment and went to the kitchen where Absylom stood, his back to her, adding curry to the simmering chicken. Hearing her, he turned and said, "Ah, for once we're both home before sunset. I've got this—" He turned around and the joy in his face seemed to drain away as if sucked up by Raven's unstated grief from Bill's passing. "It's interesting," Absylom continued, not knowing that Bill had died but fumbling to piece together what Raven knew had cracked, "funny how you chanced upon my client. I'm glad you were there for him to talk with. He's a really nice—"

"I'm dating him," Raven said.

Stunned, Absylom's dark face went blank, gave way to Raven's words.

"Your client—Drew Clarke. We've been seeing each other for two months." Raven felt life slipping away from her as when the doors of the elevator Drew had boarded slid closed. A vacant chill, as if the wind of death, enwrapped and rushed through her. "He's gone with me every night to

22

the hospital to visit Daddy. I've told him about you and me. And since Daddy Bill has died—"

The constant sadness of Absylom's eyes seemed to emit a glow that overtook his ebony face. He reached for her.

Raven stepped back. "I'm going home." Her gaze swept the room then drifted to the wooden Siva standing in the shadow of the fireplace.

"We complete our studies in June." Absylom said. "And then there is Rajas—you cannot go back to Alfreida."

Again Raven searched the orange and pink walls, like those of the houses in Jaipur. "I can't."

"What of our plans for the ashram?"

"Ashram!" Raven seemed to come alive as her universe within was disintegrating. "My father just died, and you're talking about some goddamned ashram! That's the problem with this relationship." She grabbed her head. "It's always about the ashram. The ashram! I'm sick of you and this idea of an ashram!" Her words tumbled out.

She turned to the cloth painting bearing the blue-white face of Siva and his consort, the dark and vengeful Kali, blood covering her lips. Their eyes appeared to darken as if summoning her. Raven's thoughts entered a silence of her own making. Her numbness receded.

"I don't want to go to Rajasthan."

"But you must. It is your dream, ours to share and to hold."

"Not anymore." Raven again turned to the mahogany carving of Siva dancing, the ring of fire encircling the deity. Raven's life seemed to have no beginning, no end, rather a continuous ring of tormented thoughts fueled by Alfreida's rulings. And now Daddy Bill was dead.

Absylom knitted his brows. "Everything I will build in Rajasthan sits now with us. If you go—"

Raven went to the bedroom and packed a suitcase.

"I'll be back later for the rest of my things," she said on reentering the front room.

"When?" Absylom stood from in front of the fireplace. He'd been sitting before the wooden statue of Siva.

"I don't know." She headed for the door.

He caught up to her as she put her hand on the knob, pulled the door open. Absylom caught her hand, placed the wooden carving of Siva upon her palm, and folded her fingers around it.

"Om Nama Siva." Absylom had taught Raven to recite that in an effort to silence thoughts stirred by Alfreida's criticisms. Drew had seen Raven through the ebbing of Bill's life. With Bill gone, and fears of having lost Drew encroaching, Raven chose Alfreida as a lighthouse to guide her battered ship to land. Unlike Drew, Raven refused to admit the many ways Alfreida had betrayed her and her sisters.

"Siva is you, and I am Siva." She touched Absylom's wavy black locks, and left.

When Raven arrived, Alfreida asked Teddy to leave. She took Raven to her old room, turned down the covers and lay down with her middle daughter. Hours later, the phone rang. Alfreida went downstairs. The doorbell sounded minutes afterward.

"It's Drew." Alfreida said, after knocking on Raven's door. "He's come to pay his respects."

Downstairs, Raven sat across from Drew. She thanked him for coming, and then, feeling unsure of how to proceed, "I told Absylom about us."

"I know. He called."

"When?" Raven's face grew warm.

"This evening." It had only been an hour since Raven had left Absylom. Drew added somberly, "I don't think it's a good idea for me to continue with him as my therapist. Neither does he."

"What are you going to do?"

Drew fell silent, as he had last evening in the corridor.

"I'm sorry." Raven hated having interrupted Drew's

work with Absylom. Absylom was a good therapist. "Please forgive—"

"I'm lonely," Drew said. "I'm lonely, and I like you." Raven heard Abyslom's voice: "Om Nama Siva." His words pierced the veil separating her and Drew.

"Marry me," Drew said. "Marry me, and let me take care of you. Give me something beyond work."

Raven envisioned Absylom eating alone. She forced back the sobs. Drew gently embraced her. "I'm lonely too," she said, and laid her head upon his chest.

Three days after Bill's death, Raven strained to see beyond her tears as Bill Bryant's fellow painters lowered his casket into the ground. January had slipped into February that morning. Alfreida stood to Raven's left, Drew to her right, and Teddy was next to Drew. Unbeknownst to them, Absylom observed from a distance.

Raven remained at Alfreida's throughout the winter, immersing herself in school and her counseling practicum. Drew visited each day and steadily the three made plans for Raven and Drew's wedding in June. She neither had nor allowed herself the time to think ... *for better or worse*. Raven rarely saw Absylom at school, and never at the counseling center.

In late April, Alfreida hosted Raven and Drew's engagement party. Teddy, having taken an immediate liking to Drew months earlier, introduced him to the San Francisco and Northern California legal worlds. With skill and alacrity Teddy introduced Drew's parents, a retired army colonel and his pearl-bedecked wife, to those same colleagues. The idea of doing this with Abyslom had been out of the question as far as Alfreida was concerned. And Teddy's heart pumped continuously in attendance to Alfreida's concerns.

Several hours after Teddy and Alfreida raised their champagne flutes to toast Raven and Drew's engagement,

Raven drove across the Bay Bridge to Absylom's apartment, seeking closure, release. She unlocked the door, entered the apartment, and was surprised to find Absylom there. Without a word, she turned to leave.

"No." Absylom placed his hand over hers on the doorknob.

Hours earlier at the engagement party, Raven had not understood the pendulum of her emotions. Ecstasy had engulfed her when Drew slipped his mother's engagement ring onto her finger, but she had grown sad when observing the political maneuvering of those presumably gathered to honor her and Drew. The guests, familiar with each other, all held positions in the society of law and justice. Feeling lost and out of place, Raven had longed for the serenity of the apartment she shared with Absylom, with its walls of Jaipur orange and pink. Raven was not a lawyer. Led by her own desires and losses, Raven assisted people in acknowledging and embracing their problems, their yearnings and regrets, not hiding nor denying them behind the letter of the law. Raven snatched her hand from under Absylom's, removed the dancing Siva from her pocket, and gave it back to him.

"You need to meditate," he said.

Raven grew angry. The flames of Siva encircled her. Her eyes met his and flashed a challenge. She began to undress. Absylom took her into the bedroom, laid her down, and bid entrance to her temple.

Alfreida. Daddy Bill. Teddy. The names receded into Raven's mind as the lingam of Absylom's soul held court in hers. All that Raven was and hoped to be rose and died in the silence. She closed her eyes, saw them flickering green, and herself, Raven, dancing in a ring of fire.

Raven married Drew in June. She aborted Absylom's child two months later.

⁂

Drew left for work that morning, and Raven resigned herself to the task of accompanying him to dinner in the City with his client. It would be the same restaurant where Drew took all his clients—the one in San Francisco's North End where he had taken Raven on their first date.

That evening at the restaurant, and growing weary of the conversation between Drew and his client, Raven excused herself to the ladies' room. She had flushed the toilet when a muffled cry rose from the next stall. Raven tore off some paper, bent down, and passed it underneath the divider. The woman took it. The ragged sobs continued. While drying her hands, Raven considered going back to knock on the stall door and ask if there was anything she could do, but instead she left the woman alone and slipped out the door.

Back at the table, Drew continued speaking with the client whose wife needed comforting, and Raven, somewhere between eating the Iranian osetra and Moroccan squab, lost herself in contemplation of the hollowness of her life.

The wife was a nice enough woman. While they made polite conversation, Raven's attention drifted; she caught sight of a woman with shocking-pink hair. The woman was exiting the hall that led from the ladies' room. Her round face bore lines of strain befitting the tears Raven had heard from the bathroom stall.

The woman proceeded to a table on the other side of the restaurant, sat, and unfolded her napkin. She wiped her eyes and glared at the man across from her. The lines upon her face deepened.

Raven knew that sort of anger. It rose in her each time she heard Alfreida's voice and then Kaarin's cries at night. It had risen in Raven that morning when Drew asked her to join him at dinner for his client, and again with, "Kaarin's eyes are just like yours, with hints of green that flicker each time she cries." Raven didn't hate Drew, nor Kaarin; she merely loathed what she had done at the outset of her marriage, hated that the fear stirred by Alfreida had guided her, Raven. The "now" haunted her each time she picked up Kaarin, gazed into eyes as green as her own; it spawned confusion in Raven about her own identity and her love for Drew.

⚜

Ten-year-old Raven Bryant had not been conscious of the green flecks in her eyes as she watched her mother sworn in as a superior court judge. She had been standing beside Theodore Edward Talbott, otherwise known as Teddy, her mother's longtime friend and colleague from law school.

Raven and her sisters knew Teddy Talbott as Uncle Teddy. He had been instrumental in helping Alfreida secure her judgeship and eventually brokered her appointment to the federal bench. This was no small feat for anyone, even a white man with green eyes like Teddy's.

Alfreida had demanded a divorce from Bill Bryant after giving birth to Raven's younger sister, Micki. Raven was eleven when Bill, an abstract painter, loaded his supplies and the last of his paintings into his van, and left. Alfreida then spent her free time, which was in short supply, with Teddy, who made her laugh.

Raven missed Daddy Bill. Every Friday, Bill took Raven out for ice cream or an A's game when they were playing at home in Oakland. While Raven never questioned Bill, she did wonder why he didn't bring her older sister Lauren along. "You're my baby girl," Bill always said to Raven. "And I'm your Daddy Bill." Lauren had called Bill *Daddy* too. She had also said to Raven, when angry with their mother, "Don't get confused about Daddy Bill just because Momma loves you better." Life with Alfreida, a strict disciplinarian, was trying.

⚜

Four years after Alfreida had divorced Bill, when Raven was fifteen, she had found Lauren searching Alfreida's desk drawer. "What are you doing?"

"I need my passport." Lauren, then nineteen, had kept rummaging.

"Why?"

"Because I don't intend to end up like her."

"Her who?"

"Our mother, Judge Richardson Bryant." Venom laced through Lauren's words.

Though Raven hated the way their feelings toward their mother stood between them, she secretly admired the way Lauren stood up to Alfreida. Raven was afraid of losing her older sister on that afternoon, but said, "Momma's strong."

"Yeah, but does she love us? Look at how we live." Lauren waved her hand. "She's never around. We have no father."

"There's Daddy Bill."

Lauren then said the words: "Bill Bryant's not your daddy, Raven. Neither is he mine, nor Micki's."

"That's a lie!"

Lauren came from behind the desk, took hold of Raven's shoulders, and forced her into the bathroom off their mother's study. She flipped on the light and shoved Raven in front of the mirror.

"Your eyes are green like Uncle Teddy's. Momma will never say it, but he's your daddy."

"That's not true!"

"It is." Lauren's brown eyes held tears and fears. She gripped Raven's chin and turned Raven's face toward her. "This is why I'm going to marry Kenny. I want my children to know their father."

⁂

Raven glanced across the table at Drew's client, Mr. Marshall. A balding man less than five feet tall, he wore a nicely tailored black Italian suit, a suit not unlike Drew's. It seemed ominous in contrast to Raven's fuchsia dress and the pearls about her neck and in her ears.

"It was a simple mistake." Marshall flashed his palms. "I miscalculated the profits."

"The IRS doesn't see it that way," Drew said, in the matter-of-fact manner that led his clients to stop pleading their innocence, and trust that he, knowing their guilt, would defend them vigorously.

Marshall squirmed. His wife patted his hand. Red-faced, he snatched it away.

Drew leaned in. "Now is not the time to make enemies." Legally, spouses could not be compelled to testify against their husbands or wives. They could seek divorce, however, making them fair game in the court system.

Raven looked across the table at Marshall's wife, at the crow's-feet extending from her hazel eyes, at her lips, overdone by the plastic surgeon and painted pink like the hair of the woman across the restaurant. The wife obviously loved her husband. Raven smiled despite her roiling frustration with Drew...and Kaarin's green eyes...and Kaarin's nightly crying.

Marshall continued his defense. "My friends have done much worse. I can't believe they'd send me to jail over this."

Raven wanted to reach over and slap him. *How could anyone* mislay *twenty-nine million dollars?*

Why have I never demanded Alfreida tell me who my father really is?

The pink-haired woman across the restaurant fired another loathsome glare at the man across from her. She pushed her hand further into her purse, holding something just out of sight.

Drew's client pounded his fist and rattled the crystal and dinnerware. "I'm not going to jail."

"Calm down," Drew whispered.

The sound of Kaarin's screaming filled Raven's head, and she remembered...

A month after marrying Drew, Raven's waning nausea returned. On arriving at Alfreida's for her annual Fourth of July barbecue, Raven ran inside the house and rushed past Teddy midway on the stairs and into the second floor bathroom. Minutes later and her stomach calmer, she emerged to find Teddy searching the linen closet.

"I can't seem to find the blue and white tablecloth your mother wanted."

Your mother.

The words burned in Raven's ears. Teddy routinely referred to Alfreida as "Freddy" when with friends and colleagues. To Raven and her sisters she was "your mother," the words signaling a distance, a divide that neither Raven nor Teddy had ever crossed. This Independence Day was special. Teddy had recently made Drew partner of his law firm, and Drew enjoyed working there.

Raven closed the bathroom door, stalked to the closet, and began rummaging through the piles Teddy had searched.

Her silent disapproval simmered just below boiling point. Raven had never liked Teddy, resented him for receiving the love Alfreida should have given Daddy Bill.

Teddy placed his hand upon her shoulder. She pulled away, folded and gripped her arms as if defense of something. The lessening of Raven's nausea signaled time was running out to end the pregnancy. At eleven weeks she had one week to go before special documents were needed to have the abortion.

Teddy said, "This year hasn't been easy for you. Bill's death, Absylom leaving, the wedding … "

That Teddy would venture to understand anything she had undergone stirred Raven's seething fury at him. She turned back and met green eyes that resembled hers, a reminder that Theodore Edward Talbott had gained Alfreida's love and affection, little of which had been shown to Raven and her sisters.

"Bill was your father," Teddy said with kindness. "Then you married Drew after ending what some would call a marriage with Absylom."

"Others would say it makes me an adulteress." Raven said, putting voice to Alfreida's judgment.

"Sometimes our hearts are divided. Yet to love one person more fully, we sometimes have to leave the other. It's the only way we can stay whole—otherwise we bleed to death." The light in Teddy's eyes dimmed. He had ended his marriage within months of Alfreida divorcing Bill.

The fluttering inside Raven's womb grew still.

"Bill was a good man," Teddy continued, "I'll always respect him for being there. If you ever need—"

The nausea that had subsided returned, threatening to engulf Raven. She rushed back into the bathroom, and there she remained until after the meal.

At the close of the barbecue, with Raven sitting next to Drew, Teddy led everyone in a toast to Drew's partnership with the firm. Raven smiled and clapped, all the while wondering where Absylom was at that moment, and whether she could ever attain forgiveness for having chosen to love Drew more fully. Softly she kissed Drew, opened her mind to the mahogany carving of Siva dancing that stood on the table beside her bed, and prayed that one day all would be made right.

Raven's nausea disappeared in late July, three weeks beyond the stage at which any reputable physician would perform an abortion. Unlike her elder sister, Lauren, Raven went to Alfreida.

Alfreida was with Raven the morning of the abortion, two months into Raven's marriage to Drew. In the following days, Alfreida reassured Raven she had done the right thing.

⁂

Raven smiled at the client's wife across from her and again wished for things to be set right. Alfreida would be serving Teddy dinner that night as usual.

A flicker of light from across the room caught Raven's attention. She turned and saw that the woman with pink hair had relinquished her purse and was holding the knife, its serrated blade reflecting light. In one fluid movement she stood, and lunged the blade toward her companion's neck.

"Are you fucking crazy?" The man tried to stand, but the woman had come around the table, and was behind him. She wrapped her arm about his neck. All eyes were held hostage. "Sit down before you make a fool of yourself," he whispered.

"I *was* a fool for marrying you!" The woman dug the blade's edge into the pink skin of his neck above the collar.

"Please," the man's voice dipped. The woman appeared stricken but still defiant. Without hesitation, Raven stood and made her way to the table. She was convinced this was the woman she had heard in the bathroom.

Drew followed hurriedly. "What are you doing?" he asked, in the same low voice he had used with the client back at their table.

Raven ignored him and extended her hand to the young woman with pink hair. "You don't want to do this." The women made eye contact. "I heard you crying in the bathroom stall—I handed you some tissue."

"Why do you care?" The woman, her face plump and smooth, her eyes raw with emotion, couldn't have been more than twenty-eight.

"Give yourself time."

"For what?"

"To think, and heal."

The woman pushed the edge of the knife further into the man's neck. He winced, and closed his eyes. The color drained from his skin. The breaths of the onlookers sounded desperate.

"Please," Raven said.

The woman's brown eyes darkened. Slowly she moved the knife away from the man's neck and extended the shiny blade toward Raven's palm.

"Thank you." Raven reached for her wavering hand.

Then the man blurted, "You knew I wanted a family from the start; I never lied. A family and—"

The young woman pulled back the knife, rewound her arm around the man's neck and aimed the blade at his jugular. Drew rushed from behind Raven, grabbed the woman, and shook her wrist. The knife dropped to the floor. A young waiter scurried forth, grabbed the weapon, and dashed back toward the kitchen.

Later, Raven handed the young woman a tissue and squeezed her hand. They were seated on the curb outside the restaurant. "During times like this, we have to know we're doing the best we can: trying to survive." The words flowed from Raven's lips as if under the command of a greater power. "Then maybe next time—"

"Will there be a next time?" The pink color of the woman's hair faded into the milky haze of the mid-July fog.

⁂

Raven heard Abyslom's voice: *Siva is you, and you are Siva.* The desperation she sensed in Kaarin's nocturnal crying resounded in her heart.

Alfreida had urged Raven to save her marriage. "You think Drew won't know the child isn't his? There's not that much love in the world."

But Daddy Bill, Bill Bryant...

⁂

The ambulance arrived at the restaurant. Raven accompanied the young woman to the van where, after stepping inside and saying, with a melancholy smile, "Thank you" to Raven, paramedics explained to Raven they were taking her to the hospital.

"Where will she go then?" Raven asked.

"Depends on whether the man decides to press charges."

Another van had driven him to an emergency room.

The doors closed, and the van started down the street. Raven wiped her face and went back to Drew.

The drive over the Bay Bridge into Oakland was quiet. Drew said little as he drove, and Raven sat mesmerized by the lights playing against the water. Once home, she and Drew chatted with the sitter as Drew wrote the check and reiterated his appreciation for the sitter's coming on such short notice. Dinners out, like this evening's, were a mainstay of his profession. The events of this evening, however, had been far from regular.

"No problem," the college student said, halfway through the front door. "Anisha and Emily fell asleep during the movie." She paused for a moment. "Oh, and Kaarin—she was quiet all night."

"Quiet all night?" Raven met Drew's gaze.

"Not a whimper." The sitter left.

Drew closed the door. Raven nestled her fingers in her braids and shook them. "Perhaps I'll get some sleep." She started upstairs.

"That was dangerous, what you did, trying to stop that woman," Drew stated quietly."

She climbed two more steps. Drew followed. He stopped midway up the staircase. "She had a gun in her purse."

"I know." Raven was on the landing. She turned to face him. "What you did wasn't so safe either."

Drew said nothing.

"I don't like this work you're doing," she said. Drew's clients committed corporate crimes—nothing for him to sully his hands with. He didn't handle murders or kidnappings, but instead helped businesses and individuals maintain their ill-gotten fortunes.

"It's how I feed our family." Drew climbed the steps toward her.

"I don't mean to sound ungrateful. It's just that—"

"What would you have me do?" Drew raised his palms. "Start an ashram?"

Raven's shoulders sagged. Her secret took as heavy a toll as the enormous fees Drew exacted from his clients. She retreated down the hall toward their bedroom.

Raven tossed and turned, dreaming about Alfreida, who was frantic to drown the cries of an infant, and stuffing paper into a trashcan from which the sounds intensified. The infant's screams rose to the volume of a siren. Jerked into consciousness, Raven sat up and heard Kaarin crying.

Another night came and went with Raven separated from

Drew as he slept alone in their bed. Kaarin, comforted by Raven's presence, finally slept soundly in the guest bed.

Two more days and nights came and went with Raven separated from Drew. Comforted on each occasion by Raven's presence, Kaarin slept peacefully in the arms of her mother.

On the third morning after the restaurant incident, Raven staggered into her and Drew's bedroom from which she was feeling completely exiled by the weight of sixteen weeks of sleepless nights—nearly half of a complete pregnancy. She swallowed a yawn that easily could have transformed into tears, and regarded the mahogany carving of the dancing Siva. For the length of their marriage, it had stood within a shadow's breath of their bed, first on Raven's bedside table and now in the far right corner of the bookcase overlooking her and Drew's bed. Sixteen years Raven had risen each morning and searched the deity's eyes for favor, sought repentance for what she had done to Absylom.

Drew's hands landed on her shoulders and his "I love you" claimed her attention as Absylom's had done nearly two decades earlier as she had sat in the coffee shop, transfixed by Drew's explanation of why he had entered therapy.

Raven retracted her gaze from the icon and abandoned her thoughts, redirecting to the events at the restaurant two evenings earlier. "Will the man with her press charges?"

"I doubt it," Drew said. "He came by my office yesterday, wanted to talk."

"Oh?" Raven glanced back, surprised.

"I gave him my card Monday night. He's the woman's husband. She aborted their child without him knowing."

Raven's lips trembled, wondering what Drew had sought to gain in offering the man his card. Drew kissed the space beside the strap of her gown and eased his hands down her arms, soothing her.

"I need absolution too," he whispered.

She turned in his arms, cupped her palms around his brown face, smoother than it had been last night. The scent of his cologne filled her nose. Sunlight bounced off his cuff link.

He kissed her lips, said "I love you," and left for work. No sooner had the door closed downstairs and Raven removed the clothes from the dryer, than the phone rang.

"This is Fiona. From the restaurant two nights ago." The words came at Raven after she answered.

She asked, "How did you get my number?"

"My husband, Dan, went to your husband's office this morning. They had a long talk. Dan said you were both worried about us. I suppose he just needed to talk to someone older, who's been married longer."

"How are you doing?" Raven leaned into the warm tumble of clothes on the bed.

"Fair, I suppose, all things considered." Raven didn't bring up Fiona's abortion. She asked to see Fiona, but Fiona put her off, saying she needed space to heal, as Raven had suggested.

"Look," Fiona said. "I can't talk long. They don't allow cell phones here." She laughed. "I wanted to say thank you, again. Dan said your husband's a nice man."

"It's hard being married."

Again, Fiona chuckled. "That's what Dan said your husband told him."

Fear encircled Raven as she considered the strangeness of that night's events, her conversation with Alfreida, and now this call. Fiona continued, "He told Dan that you'd just celebrated your sixteenth anniversary."

Between Drew's client briefs and Kaarin's nightly crying, the day had passed six weeks ago, but Raven had said nothing. She had awakened the next morning to find a vase of Asian lilies on the table beside her bed. The attached note read, *"With all my love, Drew."*

"Marriage is something you have to work on each day," Raven said.

"I suppose that's where Dan and I have to start. We've only been married a year. It's hard." Fiona's voice was slow, either from tiredness or the medication she had likely received.

Raven made ready to say good-bye, but Fiona said, "I thought you should know I wasn't the woman in the bathroom last night." Raven swallowed. "At first, I thought you might have said it just to make me think you cared. Then, I looked in your eyes and heard tears, like the cries of an infant. You're a good person. I suspected that the other night. Now I know it." Raven heard sniffles from Fiona's end.

Raven had heard Kaarin's screaming in the voice of the woman crying in the bathroom. She had also heard her own voice searching for Absylom. Raven had interceded into Fiona's argument with her husband out of a desire for silence.

"Fiona then said, "I loved my husband when we first married. But I didn't want the baby. I just wasn't ready for a child. I just wanted *him* for now at least—that's all."

Raven's heart sank beneath Fiona's conflicting statements and entered a land where words could not travel. She closed her eyes.

"I'd better go," Fiona said, and thanked Raven for listening.

Raven washed and folded two more loads of clothes in between preparing breakfast for Anisha and Emily, then taking them down the street to practice with their friend Sasha for the next day's soccer match. Kaarin lay asleep on the bed, encircled by the warm piles of folded clothes. Raven was on her way to the dryer for the final load when the phone rang and on lifting it from its base, heard Alfreida's voice.

"How are you?"

Raven braced the phone between her shoulder and ear as, with clothes in hand, she made her way to the bed, careful to avoid waking Kaarin."Rushed and tired, no more than usual. I was just—"

"Kaarin still not sleeping?"

Raven resisted another yawn. "She'll be fine."

"Perhaps if I came over and took her for the day," Alfreida offered, "and let you get some sleep." As Raven's eyebrows rose, Alfreida added, "Then you and Drew can join us for dinner later this evening. Teddy says he never gets to see Drew anymore." Drew was now third partner at Teddy's firm.

"I don't think so."

"Surely you need the sleep."

"I mean for dinner. Drew and I were out Monday night— over in the City. He met a client for dinner. This week's been busy." Raven separated the bath towels from lingerie, her thoughts flipping through images of the client's wife, then to the woman crying in the bathroom, and the events that followed.

What you did was dangerous, Drew had told her Monday night, and then her conversation with Fiona hours earlier. *I loved my husband . . . wasn't ready for a child . . . I wasn't the one crying in the bathroom . . .*

Raven spoke into the receiver while folding a warm towel. "Besides, it's too late to get a sitter."

"Bring Anisha and Emily. Kaarin will already be here."

"Don't you have to work?" Raven snapped.

"I cancelled my afternoon session of court, was reviewing documents my clerk completed over the weekend. Then Teddy called, suggested that I invite you, Drew, and the kids—"

"Didn't you hear me?" Raven's attention flashed to the statue of Siva dancing on the bookshelf, and then to Kaarin lying asleep amid the piles of clothes on Raven and Drew's bed, from which Raven, pulled by Kaarin's incessant crying at night, was becoming more and more estranged.

"I don't want to have dinner with you! I don't want to

see Teddy!" Raven slammed the phone down onto its base and gripped her face in horror. She had never done that to anyone, least of all her mother.

A whimper arose from Kaarin upon the bed amid clothes now growing cold. Raven turned to find the infant stirring, her tiny hands and fingers reaching into the air. She watched her youngest daughter lying upon the bed, her brown fingers reaching, her green eyes searching, wanting. Kaarin whimpered again, and then let out a cry. Raven reached for her. And then the phone rang.

Raven turned, stared at the receiver. It rang again. Lifting the baby, she crossed to the phone on the desk and saw that the number was Alfreida's. Kaarin let out a searing scream on the fourth ring. By the sixth she was bawling as if terrified.

Raven patted her daughter on the back, yet Kaarin's cries grew louder and more violent, like a tearing away. The phone continued to ring. Barely able to hold her head up, Kaarin began to sway back and forth in Raven's arms. Holding her with one hand Raven grabbed the phone, clicked it on and off, threw it onto the carpet and held Kaarin tighter than ever. The ringing stopped.

Kaarin's tiny chest beat upon Raven's heart. Her wails settled into loud sniffles then soft whimpers. Raven undid her buttons and pulled open her blouse, revealed a full and swollen nipple, and brought Kaarin to her breast. All went quiet as she lowered herself onto the chair by the window. Raven leaned back and closed her eyes.

Relief and sadness had filled Raven that spring morning when the officials swore Alfreida onto the federal bench. Teddy Talbott had stood beside Raven and clapped as Alfreida received her robe and gavel. Bill Bryant had been nine blocks away, directing the hanging of his paintings at a gallery on San Francisco's Market Street.

Teddy Talbott was Raven's father, and she knew it. Like Lauren, Absylom had spoken of it. "*He* is your father. And you need to face up to it."

"But I love Daddy Bill."

"You can love them both."

Raven had grown up knowing and loving Bill Bryant as her father. She would not allow anyone to take his place. Raven had sensed Teddy's desire to draw close to her in the years since Bill's death.

"You need to allow your heart to expand." Absylom had said.

"I can't! I won't!"

"Then you will never know peace." Absylom had said these words on the night they slept together, hours after Raven and Drew's engagement party.

Raven opened her eyes to Kaarin's, flecked with green and filled with love. The infant grew calm as she suckled, her expression intent and focused on Raven. Raven brushed the infant's cheek then caught sight of the wooden icon of Siva dancing on the bookcase across the room.

The heartbeat of Absylom's child, sixteen weeks along, had sent flutters of worry and fear through Raven's womb at twenty-four. At forty, Raven gave birth to Kaarin, who would be her last child. In the years since the abortion, Raven had often wondered if the child she aborted had her bright golden or Absylom's dark skin. She had imagined its hair to be dark and wavy like Absylom's. She brushed Kaarin's warm face, reddish-brown and smooth like Drew's.

Would the baby have had green eyes? Just then, Kaarin's green-flecked eyes fluttered open and met her mother's. Raven always confronted herself during these quiet moments. It was what she loved and hated about gazing into her last child's eyes.

Absylom's words spread through her thoughts and body. *"Siva dances only when angry. Siva dances in your eyes when you are angry—dancing and twirling, changing the world in you and me."* Siva is the destroyer, the arbiter of death after which only life arises.

Kaarin paused from suckling, and extended her tiny hand. Raven leaned down, felt her daughter's fingers touch her cheek. Easing forward she stood, and with Kaarin in her arms still suckling and looking up to her, moved toward the bookshelf as she had every morning for sixteen years. She fixed her eyes on the dancing deity held within the ring of fire, a snake about its waist. Raven stroked Kaarin's cheek a second time, seeing not only her eyes, but also the beauty of her skin, like that of red Georgia clay.

"Siva is us, and we are Siva." Siva is change—or rather our acceptance of what has been faithfully present.

The reality of Kaarin's identity slid across Raven's consciousness, diminished her need to hope, to wish that the spirit of the child she aborted sixteen years earlier lived within Kaarin. She kissed Kaarin's cheek.

⁂

Raven pulled into the driveway, turned off the ignition, took a deep breath, and got out. Reaching the back of the house, she skirted the pool, its water clear and reflecting sunlight. Now barely a month since Fourth of July, it was as sharp and luminescent as it had been that first July, weeks after Raven had married Drew and then encountered Teddy on her way out of the bathroom.

After knocking several times on the screen door, Raven tugged on the handle and found the door unlatched. She stepped inside the kitchen. The aroma of onions and porterhouse steak, Teddy's favorite, overwhelmed her senses, took her back to the day when it first became warm.

Raven was eleven, had arrived home from school and was started up the driveway toward the back of the house. She met Bill coming from around back. And then she noticed his blue van, its back doors swung open. All his belongings were inside along with the painting supplies he usually transported between home and his studio. The house Raven lived in was no longer his home.

"Where are you going?" Raven ran to meet him.

He went around her, loaded his pillow and blankets into the back of the van, then came back. He knelt down, placed his hands on her shoulders, and looked up to her.

"I'll always love you, don't forget that." He shook her as if to make the words stick, go down and settle in her heart, and then, "You're my little lump of brown sugar—with a twist of lime in your eyes." Bill's eyes had been wet as he stood to leave.

In that moment Raven became conscious of what would transfix the men significant in her life, the very thing she loathed—flecks of green in her eyes that, when in just the right light, when Raven was excited, hurt, or angry, sparkled like emeralds filled with passion—and what Raven deemed had separated her from the man she worshipped as a child, Daddy Bill.

❋ Again at her childhood home, and apprehensive about why Alfreida had left the door unlocked, Raven edged through the kitchen and headed for the staircase. A sound arose of footsteps descending. Alfreida set foot on the staircase landing between the first and second floor, and turned. Raven met her mother's look.

"I suppose you've come to apologize." Alfreida continued down, halting as she reached the last step.

Raven slid her keys into her pocket, taking a moment to summon her courage.

"I assume you won't be joining us for dinner." Alfreida let go of the banister, stepped onto the floor, and brushed past Raven who followed her into the kitchen.

"Where're the children?"

"They're with Nilini."

Alfreida slid on her oven mitts. "So much for difficulty in getting a sitter … and Drew?" She opened the oven door and reached inside for the casserole dish.

"Probably on his way home."

Alfreida lowered the dish onto the counter, then removing her mitts, closed the oven door and turned the dial to *off*.

Alfreida laid her mitts on the counter beside the hot dish.

"Why haven't you married Teddy?" Raven said.

"Are you suggesting I should?" Her mother's words were cold and sharp.

"I'm just asking in light of the fact that you left Daddy Bill to be with him."

"If I left your father to be with Teddy, as you say, then don't you think I would have married him?" Alfreida's tone bristled with indignation.

"Perhaps the real question is why did you leave Daddy Bill?" Raven moved toward her mother.

"Now I have one for you," Alfreida said. "When was the last time you spent the entire night with Drew?"

"I'm sure it hasn't been as recent as you with Teddy."

Alfreida reached out and slapped Raven. "You think dignifying your insolence will make Kaarin sleep through the night?" The sixty-year-old woman's nostrils flared.

Raven flinched, but stood her ground. "She's no longer crying."

Alfreida gave a faint chuckle and crossed her arms. "Oh, so you hung up on me and that makes everything alright?"

"Everything will *never* be alright." Raven felt herself growing weary and weak. Harboring a dead spirit was heavy business, especially when you felt it was linked to the soul of your child. "I killed my baby for you. And now it's crying out, but not through Kaarin, through me."

"Is this some psychobabble you learned in school?" Alfreida snapped, her forehead furrowed under, arched brows.

"It's what I know. I loved that child. But I'll never know what she or he would have looked like."

"And that was a decision you made."

"I made it for *you*."

Married to Drew for two months, Raven had gone to Alfreida hoping for answers; Alfreida had urged Raven to have the abortion.

Alfreida's voice had dropped to a hush. "*You* did what was needed to do to save your marriage."

"I wanted your love."

"And you think accusing me of making Kaarin cry will garner that?"

"Kaarin's been doing what I can't. What I never let myself do—cry for this child, your grandchild."

"You speak as if it's living inside of your right now."

"I feel that it is." Raven again felt phantom flutters inside her abdomen.

"This is insane." Alfreida swept past Raven.

"What I *did* was insane."

Alfreida whirled around. "Oh, so you're saying that you don't love Drew, that you never loved him, that you never came to me wanting my help?"

"I've always loved Drew, and I did want your help. I also loved the child I was carrying by Absylom."

"*That* was a mistake. And when we make mistakes we have to then make choices to correct those mistakes."

"Is that what you did when divorcing Daddy Bill—correct your mistake?" The smell of cooked onions and roast, Teddy's favorite, stirred Raven's anger. "Choose Teddy over him—over us?" Alfreida's house, the kitchen, had never felt as warm as it did that day, nor as safe as it had felt when Raven was a child.

"What I did with my life was my business." Alfreida's tenor changed; her eyes grew fixed and stern. "I complained to no one. And you girls never went lacking."

"Except for your love."

The operating room's antiseptic smell should have grown stale but instead cut through the years and filled her nose as it did each night when Kaarin cried out. Raven felt herself grow numb, as she had when being anesthetized for the abortion.

"*Om Nava Siva,*" Raven had whispered as Alfreida left the room that day, a string of rosary beads dangling from her hand. "I don't want to go through with this, but I love Drew."

She repeated those same words now. *Om Nava Siva, if only for Siva to stomp upon their heads and deliver absolution.*

Raven inhaled the aroma of onions and roast. She didn't want Kaarin in bed with her and Drew. She wanted to continue imagining, hoping that Kaarin was the child she had aborted—hers by Absylom—now reincarnated, and no part of Drew. But the crying had worn her down. Kaarin's wails held Raven's unshed tears for the child she aborted.

Raven's desperation and fury stirred to a new level. "We gave up so much for you." Her thoughts flashed to her elder sister Lauren's botched abortion, from which Lauren had nearly died. "It's amazing that Lauren has even had any children by Brian."

"I never told her to run off with that fool, Kenny."

"She took up with him trying to get out from under your thumb." And then there were Raven's own bouts with postpartum depression that had resolved after Anisha, and then Emily's birth. It had worsened upon delivering Kaarin.

"I will never let Anisha, Emily, or Kaarin endure what you put us through."

"Don't be so haughty," Alfreida said. "The road between hope and reality runs wide. All parents have plans for their children."

"And you haven't answered my question."

"To which you know the answer."

"Why didn't you love Daddy Bill, us, like you do Teddy?" Raven applied a new tactic.

"Why did you leave Absylom?" Alfreida shot back. "And don't tell me I made you do it."

"You never liked Absylom."

"You were a grown, twenty-four-year-old woman."

"I needed your help—"

"And I gave it."

"You threatened to disown me if I married Absylom."

"I was never going to support your following a man into the Indian desert to build some sort of temple—throwing your life away. No. You were my child. I wanted you safe."

"You wanted me here with you, in *your* world," Raven said.

"I wanted the best for you."

"You wanted me *without* Absylom's child, and I wanted your—"

"Absylom Mugezi has been out of our lives for sixteen years. Why are we talking about this now?"

"I killed my child sixteen years ago for you—the same length of time Daddy Bill's been dead!" Raven sobbed. "Sixteen—the number of weeks since I had Kaarin—sixteen weeks that she's been crying."

"You did what was needed to save your marriage."

"I needed your love! Just like now," she said, choking on her words. "I need you to tell me why I have this child's voice inside of me, this infant crying, why I want to cry and can't."

"I don't know what you're talking about."

"I'm mourning my child, but there's another death around me. I feel it."

Alfreida started away, but Raven followed and tugged at Alfreida's arm.

"Did you want me? Or am I just imagining something? Was I the reason you left Daddy Bill—your mistake? Who am I!"

"You're my daughter." Alfreida whipped around. "*My* child." She hit her chest. "That's all that matters."

The screen door opened, and Teddy stepped inside.

Raven turned to him, her eyes wet with tears meeting his, green and sparkling like she knew hers were.

Raven ran past him, fearing herself about to crumble, life as she knew it and as she knew herself, transforming, ebbing into something new.

As she reached her car, she heard her mother's voice

resounding from inside the house.

"I will not tell her! I will not!"

"But Freddy—"

"Don't *but* me. Raven is *my* child. Mine! Do you hear me, Teddy? She's my child." A door slammed.

·�֍·

Anisha and Emily were asleep in their beds as Raven turned from the dancing Siva upon the bookshelf and looked at Drew lying in bed. His arm was entwined about Kaarin, her small warm body held close to his heart. Father and daughter were asleep. It was midnight.

The infant opened her eyes, and smiled in the dim light of the lamp. Kaarin was Raven's child, but not the one fathered by Absylom. And Alfreida was a Chinese box, some of whose doors remained closed, while others opened to secrets locked behind walls that came in and out of view. Her sphinx-like ways came and went. But Kaarin's nighttime crying, constant since birth, had ceased.

Kaarin's eyes flickered green. Raven leaned down, and as she had earlier that afternoon, allowed the child's fingers to touch her cheek. Amid the quiet surrounding them, tears for the child she would never see christened Raven's mournful face and slid between by the tiny fingers of her last child.

Siva is you, and you are Siva.

Keeper of Secrets

The letter Lahni received that morning had read:

> This letter is to inform you that Dr. Karl Schreiber, psychoanalyst, has died. In accordance with the terms of his will, I, William J. Roberts, executor of Dr. Schreiber's estate, have destroyed all records of Dr. Schreiber's work with clients, former and present. Should you have further questions, please call 212-557-92…

Eight years had passed since Lahni had seen her analyst, Karl Schreiber. Eight years since she had married Nwoyé. Lahni had been a thirty-year-old, newly licensed psychoanalyst, while Schreiber was a seventy-one-year-old Holocaust survivor.

Lahni folded the letter and remembered her final session with the last person who knew her secret.

⚜

"Are you sure you want to marry him?" Schreiber had asked, concerning Nwoyé, Lahni's then-fiancé, who was born and raised in Nigeria.

"He loves me."

"Amos loves you too."

Lahni and Amos Morgan had been childhood friends, and then had trained at an analytic institute in upstate New York during the eighties.

"I feel safe with Nwoyé."

"And you don't feel safe with Amos, who is sighted?"

"Are you implying I shouldn't marry Nwoyé because he's blind?"

Lahni's words resonated within. Taking in her words she met the blue clarity of her analyst's eyes. Karl Schreiber had listened to Lahni's thoughts twice, and often three times a week for more than six years.

"Have you told Nwoyé what happened in Nigeria?"

"No. And I don't plan to." When she was fifteen, three women had chased Lahni, an African American, into a dense forest surrounding the village of Ampu, in Nigeria. They had intended to circumcise her.

"What frightens you about his knowing what happened?"

"I killed someone."

Lahni and Schreiber had discussed the incident a thousand times over. On each occasion, Schreiber defended Lahni's actions: "You were frightened—you thought they were going to kill you."

Lahni, unsure of who she was when she had acted, always responded, "How do you know I won't do it again?"

Lahni had also witnessed murder. Once, when she was eight years old, she had begged her mother for ice cream, and they went to the grocery store near her home in Mt. Vernon. Her father had been away for the summer—as in past summers—gathering blood samples from various tribes of West Africa for his genetics research. Escaped convicts staged a robbery while they were at the store. Her mother shielded Lahni when the convicts began shooting hostages.

In Lahni's mind, the woman in Ampu with the knife became one of the convicts from the store. Years later, her father explained that the women had wanted to circumcise Lahni—something he didn't condone. Like Dr. Schreiber, Lahni's father saw her actions as those of a child who was afraid. Lahni didn't see it that way.

"Nwoyé offered to tell me how he lost his eyesight. I told

him I didn't need to know." Schreiber nodded. "He thanked me for not needing to know." She spoke quietly, "My secret is safe."

"But from whom?"

Lahni had stared into her hands, and ended her last session with Schreiber never having answered. She married Nwoyé the next day.

On the morning of their eighth anniversary, Lahni considered the secrets between her and Nwoyé, and what they said about their marriage and her husband—and most of all, what they said about her. Nearly a decade had passed since that last session with Dr. Schreiber.

Nwoyé was a good and faithful husband. A financier with contacts around the world, he often traveled on his Citation 10 to meet with heads of state in Kenya, Rangoon, or any of the innumerable places where he provided seed money for start-up companies. Nwoyé's sense of independence had beguiled Lahni at the outset of their relationship. He welcomed Lahni to join him on his travels, but Lahni clung to her analytic practice.

On their first anniversary, Nwoyé said of Lahni to their friends, "I have married a keeper of secrets."

Karl Schreiber, the custodian of Lahni's secrets, was now dead.

Lahni blotted out the memories of her last session with Dr Schreiber and slid closer to Nwoyé. Across from her, Amos smiled.

"Happy anniversary." Nwoyé kissed her hand.

Amos's wife, Nicole, seated beside Amos and across from Nwoyé, smiled too. "I can't believe that eight years have passed since I introduced you two."

"Hear, hear." Amos raised his champagne flute.

Amos and Lahni worked alone in their Victorian painted lady on Union Street. On learning that Lahni was to marry

Nwoyé, Amos had asked her to join him in his analytic practice in San Francisco. The last eight years had been like old times at the analytic institute back in New York—Amos and Lahni chatting about their practice before and after sessions, and during lunchtimes as well.

Lahni and Amos's years as colleagues had unearthed aspects of themselves that not even Lahni's sessions with Schreiber could rival. Lahni loved her husband, but she treasured Amos.

She returned Amos's smile. Then the commotion began.

"This is my body; I'll do what I want with it!" screamed a woman with pink hair several tables over.

"Not when it's *my* child!" the man across from her cried. Suddenly, the woman was holding his neck and had a knife to his throat.

Nwoyé clutched Lahni's hand. "What's happening?" While Nicole leaned across and described the outburst, Lahni met Amos's look again. Her memories triggered by the violence, she found herself reliving the incident in Ampu.

⁂

It was a hot June day when Lahni rushed into the bush surrounding the African village. Tears mixed with sweat stung her cheeks. She ran in zigzag fashion to evade the three women pursuing her. Lahni raced into a clearing and scurried to the side opposite the waterfalls. She hid behind a tree.

On reaching the clearing, the women scattered in three directions. The one with the knife approached the tree behind which she stood. The woman scanned the area, turning until her back was to Lahni.

Lahni hefted a rock, crept up on the woman, and pounded her skull with it. The woman fell to her knees. She dropped the knife. Lahni stared at her would-be attacker, stricken by the thought that her mother would have been this woman's age had her mother lived.

Lahni didn't remember picking up the blade. Minutes

later, she found herself standing over the woman, whose blood seeped from her side into the earth, which absorbed the blood like a dark sponge.

When the other two women returned to the clearing and saw their friend, they began to wail. A chill cut through Lahni, sharp as the blade that had pierced the woman's side.

That same coldness passed through her as she witnessed the woman with pink hair holding the knife to the man's neck.

Nwoyé tightened his grip on Lahni's hand.

Shaking her head and returning to the present, she found Amos's attention still fixed on her. Her eyes locked with his. Amos reached for her hand, but she snatched it away.

At home that night Lahni moved on top of Nwoyé and caressed his neck. Driven by the motion of their bodies—his dark brown and hers sienna—she traveled deeper into the wilderness of her thoughts. Images of hibiscus and flowing streams amongst trees, which extended toward the sun, surrounded their bodies.

Nigeria.

Then the knife appeared, as it had in the restaurant. The second woman, the beautiful one who wore a fuchsia dress and pearls about her neck, approached the woman with the knife, trailed by a man wearing a black suit, and who seemed terribly concerned.

The man shrieked and the woman with pink hair jerked his neck back, pressed the blade against his flesh.

The nicely dressed man rushed around the table to the woman with the knife. "Like my wife said, you don't want to do this." The knife dropped to the floor.

And then there was Amos looking into Lahni's eyes.

❀ Cold and shivering, Lahni slid from Nwoyé's body, and pulled the sheet over herself.

"What is wrong?" Nwoyé's Yoruban accent was softly layered with British undertones. His words hung in the air.

"I wonder what made the woman in the restaurant want

to kill the man."

"Are you certain that is what she wanted?"

"No." Lahni had a flash of the woman in Ampu with the knife. She had seemed so certain of her task when speaking to the women with her. But Lahni had not heard their exchange.

Lahni threw back the covers, slipped into her gown, and went to the bathroom. She turned on the light and stared at her brown eyes in the mirror.

Murderess. Her throat tightened. The gunman in the store had aimed his rifle at Lahni. She closed her eyes.

Nwoyé entered the bathroom, and stood behind Lahni like the tall man who had guarded his wife in the fuchsia dress. The pearls she had worn reminded Lahni of her mother's pearls, worn to the grocery store the day they went for ice cream.

Nine hours had passed before the gunmen started shooting hostages. When Mt. Vernon police stormed the store, Lahni's mother lay dead, like the woman in Ampu would seven years later.

Lahni caught her breath.

"What do you see?" Nwoyé pressed his naked body against her back. She felt herself choking.

"There is nothing that could make me stop loving you," he whispered. Her eyes remained closed.

"Where are you right now, Nwoyé? Please take me there."

Nwoyé drew close and began describing his world. "There is a field ... between the woods and the savanna ... between the forest and the plains, where the breath of Olodumare blows." He kissed her neck. "The earth is dry, but life abounds there. Oya's waters drench its thirst."

Lahni leaned her head back upon Nwoyé's shoulder and inhaled the picture spreading on the canvas of her eyelids — clear and crackling streams nestled in the dense forest, verging on the Nigerian plain.

"This place—it is called Eba Odan. Let me take you there." Nwoyé slid the gown from her body, caressing her bare skin.

They went to bed, Nwoyé traveling inside Lahni again, and she entered a surreal abyss forested by people and animals whom she felt like a beast for having killed.

The next morning, Lahni opened the office door and looked up to meet Amos's concerned eyes.

"Was Nwoyé okay once you got home?" He pushed open the door and followed her inside. "He seemed agitated during the restaurant debacle."

Lahni laid her briefcase on the desk and flipped it open. Amos, beside her, reached for her hand as he had done last night at the restaurant. Again she pulled away, and began rifling through client notes. She dug out a pen and pad, then slammed her briefcase shut.

The face of the woman in Ampu appeared in her mind. The smell of blood filled Lahni's nose.

"Something's bothering you. I saw it the moment you came into the restaurant last night—and again when that scene broke out."

Lahni took a deep breath. "Dr. Schreiber, my analyst at the Institute—he died. The woman in the restaurant with the knife reminded me of a client I discussed with him several times."

"Care to elaborate?"

"I've got a client like that now," she hedged.

"Which one?"

"It's a new client." She attempted to move past him, but he quickly caught her arm, then just as quickly let go. He picked up a pad from her desk.

"There's a psychiatrist on College Avenue in Berkeley." He began writing.

"He's black—out of residency for five years—as good as I am, if not better." With an air of resignation, he tore off the paper and handed it to Lahni.

"Tell him you're my partner." Amos walked to the door. "And if you choose—" he said, turning to her, "let me know how it goes."

Hostage once again. Lahni stared at the name and number. *Where could the Berkeley psychiatrist take her?*

❧ Lahni was midway across the lower deck of the Bay Bridge when she decided to shift into the faster-moving far left lane. Her appointment with the psychiatrist was in less than thirty minutes. Preparing to move, she glanced into her left side mirror. Rather than seeing an open lane or a car approaching from behind, Lahni saw the woman she had killed in Ampu. And the woman was smiling. Lahni's mother then appeared beside her. The knife from the restaurant— the one Lahni had seen pointed toward her when she made love to Nwoyé—hung between the women. Shocked, Lahni began drifting right, heard a loud honk from the car in the far right lane, approaching from behind. She gripped the wheel and tried to shake herself free of the vision.

❧ Dr. Reynard Williams's office was nothing like Lahni's. African masks hung on the back of Lahni's door, and her walls were a soft shade of ecru carefully chosen to convey a sense of warmth and safety. Dr. Williams's stark white walls were graced by images of the Buddha during the various stages of enlightenment. The afternoon breeze stirred the curtains on the window nearest the intricately detailed fireplace. A bronze statue of the Buddha stood on the mantle.

"Thank you for seeing me on such short notice." Lahni had not assumed the role of patient in eight years.

Dr. Williams smiled. "Amos introduced me to the community when I moved here five years ago." Amos had not mentioned Williams until that morning, six hours earlier.

Dr. Williams laid down his pen. "So what seems to be—"

"I don't need any medication," Lahni said abruptly, as she met the psychiatrist's gaze. "Last night there was an incident in a restaurant. My husband and I were celebrating our anniversary."

Dr. Williams gave a soft smile.

"My partner, Amos, and his wife, Nicole, were our guests. Nicole was the one who introduced me to Nwoyé."

Lahni briefly described the incident, finishing with, "If the other woman hadn't intervened, she would have cut his throat. But the woman in the fuchsia dress didn't do it alone. Her husband was right behind her."

The curtain fell still.

"She was a beautiful black woman with eyes that sparkled. And then there was this man with her, maybe her husband," Lahni explained. "He never lost sight of her—or the knife."

The bronze Buddha reclaimed her attention, and her thoughts drifted to Amos. Lahni liked the attention Amos gave her, but afraid and ashamed of her actions in Nigeria, she recoiled from Amos's displays of affection. She had declined his proposal during the spring before their last year of training at the institute.

Hurt and despondent, Amos had traveled to Ghana for the summer. He met Nicole, a Parisian, while trekking outside of Kumasi. He married her that fall.

Lahni pulled herself from her reflective trance and picked up where she left off, describing how they had been seated during the previous evening's incident. "Nwoyé was beside me, facing Nicole. She described the incident to Nwoyé as it played out." Lahni pulled at her fingers.

"Amos was beside Nicole, across from me. He never turned away. He looked at me the whole time. That's when I remembered everything, like it was happening all over— the women in Ampu, Nigeria; they tried to circumcise me." Lahni turned to the window. Somehow I've always thought of those women when I picture the gunmen who killed my mother." She recounted her mother's death, then said, "I killed the woman who tried to circumcise me."

Williams remained silent but alert as Lahni explained.

"My father was a physician who taught genetics. Every summer of my life he traveled to villages along the West Coast of Africa, gathered blood samples, and examined them for various genetic sequences unique to each African tribe. His dream was to isolate them for all the tribes so that African Americans could trace their lineage simply by submitting their DNA for analysis.

"Momma and I had never accompanied him. Each May after he'd turned in students' grades, I'd beg him to take me and Momma. I always thought it was Daddy who didn't want us to go. Eight years after Momma was killed, I implored him not to leave me with Momma's sister Lena. He took me along." Lahni folded her arms across her chest, rubbed her arms.

"Four years after everything had happened, when I was preparing to leave for college, he told me it was Momma who didn't want to go. She hadn't approved of his work, couldn't understand why he'd chosen to teach instead of practice medicine like her father."

Lahni's chin jutted upward. "He also said that after Momma had died, he fell in love with someone. That summer I went with him to Ampu, he asked the woman to marry him. Her name was Kaeki. She lived in Ampu." Lahni's voice cracked, but she forged on.

"Kaeki always took me on walks, made me things. I liked her. After everything happened and we were back home, Daddy tried to explain that by tribal custom, Kaeki must have been circumcised, and I would have had to undergo the same procedure for her to feel safe marrying him. 'Circumcised women feel threatened by those who are not,' Daddy told me. He knew of their customs, but not about Kaeki or her plans. She wasn't with the three women who came after me to do her bidding. Daddy was certain they were working in her honor. It was their way."

Lahni searched the psychiatrist's eyes, then turned to the Buddha on the mantel behind him. "My husband is Nigerian. He's also blind. I've never resented that, it's just that sometimes … "

Through the window Lahni regarded the tree on the edge of the parking lot. She hesitated, then said, "Nwoyé's eyes are open when we make love. Mine are closed."

"Would you like to open them?" Williams asked.

"Yes," she murmured, adding, "I love Nwoyé. He has secrets too, but I don't want this one between us."

"How might holding your eyes open while making love help you achieve that?"

"It will let me see—him loving me—me loving myself—my mother—" Lahni lowered her head and retraced the path she had initially cut open.

"Amos met Nicole the spring after I refused to marry him. She had been studying painting at the Sorbonne. Nwoyé was there too."

"Your husband was a painter before he lost his sight?"

"A hobby. Nwoyé loves art."

"Still, it must have been difficult losing his ability to paint."

"Nwoyé never said. He lost his sight before I met him. I never let him tell me about it; I never needed an explanation."

"Like you didn't accept Amos's proposal."

Lahni tensed. She had not considered her actions in that frame.

"Do Amos or Nicole know how Nwoyé was blinded?"

Lahni again turned her attention toward the window and the sunshine and trees … and the memories that lay beyond Reynard's office.

❉ Amos had called her each week after he and Nicole moved to Berkeley. Lahni and Amos had been speaking daily when Nicole introduced Lahni to Nwoyé at the United Nations Building.

The following day Amos took Lahni to lunch. "We don't know how he lost his sight," Amos said of Nwoyé. "He was fine eight months ago in San Francisco when we saw him at the Museum of Modern Art."

Amos sighed, gripped his mug tighter. "Nwoyé won't tell Nicole anything. Nicole studied painting with him at the Sorbonne for three summers before I met her. A month after she and I settled in Berkeley, she saw him at the Asian Art Museum in San Francisco. He started sending us tickets to art shows around the Bay Area. When I have clients to see, Nicole goes alone."

He picked up his mug and looked pointedly at Lahni. "Nwoyé comes from a traditional Nigerian family. His elder brother never would have approved of him marrying Nicole. Nwoyé assures me they'll receive you." Amos took Lahni's hand. "I'd love to have you join me in my practice in San Francisco."

⁂

The breeze died, and the curtains settled against the white walls of the office. Once more Lahni shifted her attention back to the Buddha with its eyes half-closed, half-opened. "I've never worried about Nwoyé being unfaithful," she said as she described meeting him. "He made me feel warm and safe." Then softly, "I liked that he couldn't see me. No chance for judgment."

"Do you ever wish your husband could see you now? Or want him to tell you how he lost his sight?"

"Nwoyé's all I have. I don't care what he's has done, who he may have killed—" Lahni stopped short. The clients whose businesses Nwoyé funded and advised often had shadowy backgrounds. Past regimes had left them with wealth that required shelter. American politicians also found refuge and fortune in Nwoyé's connections.

Without giving Williams the opportunity to question her statement, Lahni quickly changed the subject, describing what had happened on the Bay Bridge on her way to the appointment. "I saw her face in my side-view mirror—the woman from Ampu. My mother was there too, and the knife from last night hung between them. When it dropped, my mother picked it up."

"What do you think that means?"

"I need to speak to my husband."

The Buddha's eyes were neither closed nor open. Lahni would see Williams next week.

❋ Lahni handed the tollbooth attendant three dollars, and started off. Her cell phone rang and she flipped it open.

"I hate to bother you." Amos sounded harried and tense, like he had during his first year in California. "The new bipolar client I took on last week—he jumped off a building."

"Is he alive?"

"Barely."

Starting a new life in Berkeley with Nicole, a Parisian by birth and temperament, had presented Amos with many challenges, as had building a new practice in San Francisco. Although Amos and Lahni had grown up together, they had never lived outside New York. Both felt like an exile without the other nearby.

Amos sounded beleaguered. "It was only three floors. But…"

"What can I do to help?"

"There's a consult I agreed to assess at Langley Porter, if you have the time. Where are you now?"

"Across town." Lahni said nothing of the Berkeley appointment. "What's the room number?"

Committing the number to memory, she sped back to San Francisco, conducted the session, and delivered her report to the floor nurse. Lahni then dialed Nwoyé at his office on California Street, and headed home.

As she entered the lobby of the Jackson Street building housing their condo, Lahni saw Amos rise from the sofa by the elevator.

"How are you?" She approached him, placing her hand upon his arm.

"I don't know what happened today," he said, as if to himself.

"How's your client?"

He shook his head sadly. "I can't go home tonight, Lahni." She could tell that he wanted to be with her.

"But Nicole's worried." After dialing Nwoyé, Lahni had called Nicole and told her what happened.

"You called her?!"

Just then, the elevator door opened and Nwoyé stepped off wearing his silk robe and holding his cane in front of him. A vine of desire entangling the three spread throughout the lobby.

"I didn't know you were home." Lahni hurried toward him.

"I've been waiting." He reached out and she took his hand.

"Amos and I were discussing a client."

"I know," Nwoyé's voice was stern. "Nicole called me." "She wants to know when Amos is to arrive home. I came down when the doorman rang up and said a gentleman was in the lobby."

"I thought we might offer him dinner." Lahni turned to Amos, while holding tight to Nwoyé's hand. Amos's shadowy eyes darkened. What once felt obscure was now inescapable.

Amos approached Lahni beside Nwoyé, her fingers entwined with those of the one who could not see her, whose pulsating thread of secrecy had kept her safe. "Thank you for seeing my client," Amos leaned forward. He kissed Lahni's cheek, and without addressing Nwoyé, said "but I do need to go." He left, and something went with him.

The door to the lobby closed. Lahni turned to Nwoyé. And before she could speak, he said, "I need you to be honest with me. Do you love Amos because he can see you? I need to know."

Stunned into silence, Lahni searched his eyes, empty of sight. Finding only love and compassion there, she answered, "I killed a woman. I was fifteen," she continued in a voice nearly breaking. "I was in Nigeria."

Nwoyé claimed her hand and indicated for her to move toward the elevator.

"Do you want to know what happened?" Lahni asked as they stepped on.

"No, other than to know that you are safe, and that nothing haunts you about this now."

Lahni took in a deep breath. "I am very safe. Thank you for giving me refuge." The elevator closed, and they started up.

The elevator came to a slow halt upon nearing the penthouse.

"Cook has prepared your favorite," Nwoyé said as the doors opened and Lahni led him off. "Warm seafood salad with split pea soup and garlic bread. And for myself... " He slid his arm between Lahni's and her side, yielded his elbow to the curve of hers. "For myself, I shall feast upon the pleasure of dining with you. I will massage your neck and shoulders as you eat. You may feed me anything you desire."

Nwoyé's words betrayed a knowledge of not only how much a person's hidden truths, however treacherous or sad, defined them, served as the glue holding all intact, but also bound that person to those entrusted with holding their confidence, keeping their secrets.

Lahni fell asleep next to Nwoyé later that night. The woman from Ampu returned, and again she held the knife. But this time, Lahni's mother stood beside her. The woman handed the knife to Lahni's mother, who extended it to Lahni before the two shadows retreated into the oblivion of memory.

Lahni reached out into the darkness, and closed her hand around the blade. She opened her eyes and instead of pain, felt Nwoyé's arms around her.

As Far as I Can See ...in a Day

The accident had cut an indelible path to the memory that revolved in Sahel's mind: Titus's troubled demeanor. Carl's judgmental stare, as if saying to Titus, "You caused this." The two boys shuffled through the doorway and onto the porch, Titus's eyes never leaving Sahel until he passed through.

Cecile, Titus's mother, hastened to Lillian and pried her fingers, nearly white, from about Sahel's thin, dark arms. "She's your daughter," she chided Lillian. Cecile loved Sahel. "Don't keep treating her this way. One day she won't be little." Lillian's eyes widened. Cecile seemed to know of the punishments she leveled on Sahel.

Cecile said, "Sahel and Titus are all we have that can live beyond us. We need to cherish them." Cecile's husband Howard was strict with Titus. Howard crossed the line too.

Lillian relinquished Sahel's arm. Sahel ran back to the kitchen, knelt upon the floor, and peeked through the space between the door and the wall. She saw Cecile embrace Lillian—two women, neighbors, who over the years of watching their son and daughter play, had become closer than sisters.

Cecile backed away and administered hard words. "If you don't want Sahel, give her to me, Lillian. I'll raise her with Titus. Do right by her. If you lay another hand on her, so help me God, I'll take her from you."

Sahel looked at the welts on the skin of her arms, dark like Carl's. Sahel's mother never invited Carl's mother to join her and Cecile. A peacemaker, and fair-skinned like Lillian Ohin, Cecile Denning often spoke with Carl's mother and worked with her on parish committees. Cecile liked Mrs. Pierson, Carl's mother, but never disrupted her daily lunches with Lillian by suggesting Lillian invite another person. Cecile and Titus's visits were Sahel's reprieve. They were also a time when Sahel could invite Carl to play.

The following month of that summer when Sahel was ten, Cecile Denning and her husband Howard went to visit her sister who had just delivered her first child. On the way to the hospital, an eighteen-wheeler slammed into Cecile and Howard's car as they entered the New Jersey Turnpike. Both were killed. An orphan, Titus was sent to live with his father's brother—Cecile's brother-in-law, in New Jersey, near where Cecile's sister lived.

5:00 a.m.
Titus pressed his lips against Sahel's hair. She dug her head deeper into the softness of the pillow. "I love you," he whispered, and then left for work.

The door closed, and Sahel opened her eyes into a darkness thicker and deeper than had existed with her eyes closed. She wished she had taken more of the capsules that silenced her heart. Eighteen months had passed since the accident. Sahel was blind.

8:00 a.m.
The phone rang, then the housekeeper handed Sahel the receiver.

"Hi, Carl," she said, with forced *bonhomie*.

"Where's Titus?" Carl said, after greeting her.

"In surgery. Didn't you see him at the hospital?"

"My patient spiked a temp. I cancelled my case—thought we might head for the Lake."

Carl called every morning. He didn't call until eleven on Wednesdays, their day to walk along Lake Merritt.

"I can't go today, Carl."

"Has Titus said something?" Titus knew of Sahel's Wednesday outings with Carl. "No, I'm meeting with Reynard Williams," Sahel said.

"Are you thinking about going back to work?"

"No." Sahel was in no condition to see clients. Their Wednesday walks were the only time she left the house now. "He wants to consult with me on a case."

"You know, we can't keep putting off your surgery. You can't go on like this. Perhaps someone else should do it."

"I want you to do it. It's just that—"

"You're scared; that's normal. I'd be surprised if you weren't."

Sahel choked back tears threatening to spill onto her ebony face. "Believe me, I want my sight back." Blindness wasn't her only problem.

Six months ago, Sahel had swallowed pills that stopped her heart. In the emergency room, when the defibrillator failed to jump-start her sinus rhythm, Titus, her husband, threw down the paddles, pressed his bare hands to her chest and got her heart beating. Carl had continued squeezing the intubation balloon while reciting the rosary. Sahel loved Carl like a brother. Carl was also Sahel's neurosurgeon.

"I'm going to have the surgery. I just need time to understand why this happened—who I am because of it—and how to get through. I need to make things right—just in case." The surgery to restore Sahel's sight came with risks. She might die.

"Maybe we can walk the Lake on Friday," she offered.

"That's Titus's afternoon off."

"Yes, but he's lecturing to a group of residents."

Carl became brusque. "He needs to cancel it and take you to the Lake."

Belligerent and sometimes arrogant, Titus, a heart surgeon, opposed Sahel's surgery, yet he asked her to leave her cane home when they went out. Sahel, for her part, loved Titus in a way she hadn't known before the accident.

Blindness had forced her to accept Titus—and his love.

"Can we talk later this evening, Carl?"

"I won't be home."

Sahel, and everyone acquainted with Carl, knew he would one day make a wonderful husband. Sahel's blindness was exposing their deepest wounds.

"What's her name?" Sahel asked, to lighten the mood. "When will I meet her?"

"When you can look at her and tell me that she loves me as much as I love you." Sahel forced herself to breathe. "You're my best friend. I need to feel you looking at me," Carl said.

"Reynard's coming at noon. I need to get dressed." Sahel lacked words to acknowledge what their world didn't make space for. What in the past had taken minutes now exhausted her.

She clicked off the phone, her lifeline and an instrument she feared communicated words she hadn't meant.

Noon

As a practicing psychologist, Sahel had welcomed Reynard Williams, a psychiatrist, into the Oakland-Berkeley medical community by inviting him to lunch. The two began referring clients and providing each other with consultation, when they learned they shared similar philosophies and approaches. After the accident, Sahel transferred to Reynard as many of her clients as he could accommodate. After placing the remainder with other therapists, she mailed her license to the state board, effectively relinquishing her ability to practice psychotherapy. Carl notified Reynard Williams of Sahel's action. Reynard FedExed a letter to the board that explained her recent trauma:

> Sahel Denning, PhD, is an excellent psychotherapist to whom I have referred many clients. Due to her recent trauma, she is in no state of mind to make

such a decision as to whether she should surrender
her license to practice psychotherapy.

The board refused Sahel's request, saying that she lacked
documentation confirming she had undergone a year of
psychotherapy. Sahel hadn't spoken to Reynard Williams
since she became blind.

Reynard led Sahel into their stroll along the lake. "I'm
grateful for what you did with the board," she said quietly.

He patted her hand, which rested on his arm. "My actions
were truly narcissistic. I wanted to be able to legally call on
you for consultation."

They continued walking Lake Merritt, the sun warming
Sahel's face. Reynard said, "I hope you don't think I came
to you because my client's husband is blind," a fact that had
actually piqued Sahel's curiosity.

She offered calm silence as Williams relayed his client's
first session. "She was at a restaurant over in the City. A fight
broke out between a pair at another table. A woman tried
to stab the man sitting across from her. According to my
client, the woman tried to cut his throat with a steak knife.
Another man stopped her—the husband of the woman who
intervened."

Sahel leaned in, paying close attention. Reynard went on
to explain that the woman with the knife had had pink hair.
"Kind of spiked. Definitely out of place for the restaurant—
dark windows, intimate—North Beach."

Sahel and Reynard approached the bridge connecting
Lake Merritt to Kaiser Center. "My client and her husband
were celebrating their eighth anniversary. Another couple
was with them. The husband of that pair was Amos
Morgan." Sahel knew Amos Morgan. An analyst, he lived
in Berkeley and practiced in San Francisco.

"My client and Amos are partners. They share ownership
of a Victorian on Union Street. They're pretty close."

Reynard told her he had consulted with Amos on several

of the clients he had inherited from Sahel. During these sessions, Amos alluded to his own marital problems. Amos never mentioned his partner, Lahni. Amos also never spoke of Lahni's husband Nwoyé.

Sticky warmth penetrated Sahel's fingers from Reynard's arm. "My client said that when the fight broke out, Amos never looked to see what was happening." Reynard repeated to Sahel what the client had said in session. *He was sitting right across from me. His eyes never left me—like the husband of the woman who'd intervened, Amos stayed attentive...I remembered what they tried to do to me in Nigeria. I was almost circumcised.*

Sahel slowed her pace. Reynard told of his client's experience with tribal circumcision customs. "Three women chased her into the woods, were going to put her through the procedure. She killed the one with a knife. My client's father had fallen in love with one of the village women. Was going to marry the woman."

"How old was she?"

"Fifteen."

Sahel's father, Essien, was Ghanaian. He had never spoken to her about the ritual.

"That's when I realized Amos is giving my client what her husband never can. Amos can *see* her."

Sahel recalled Carl's words. *I need to look into your eyes— see you looking back at me.*

Reynard continued. "The morning after the incident in the restaurant, Amos saw that she was troubled. He gave her my name and number."

"Does he know what happened to her in Nigeria?"

"No. For her, it's not what she was subjected to; rather it's what she did. She feels guilty for killing the woman, and harbors it as a secret. In her mind, she's a criminal who hasn't served her time."

"She's serving the time of her own judgment for protecting her ability to experience joy, "Sahel remarked.

"And that's the very thing she lacks, especially when with her husband." Reynard's words were deadpan.

Sahel considered the affective aspects of circumcision, how it numbs a woman from experiencing a source of pleasure, silences one's physical and emotional voices.

Sahel had refused to let Titus tell anyone, except her father and Carl, what happened the night of the accident. She made the three men agree that the formal story would be that Sahel had fallen down the stairs in her father's home and hit her head.

Reynard revealed more of his client's life. "I think her husband has money. He's in finance, has a Citation 10, does business in Beijing, Mexico City, Dubai. He's all over the world, despite his blindness."

The noon sun of early autumn warmed Sahel's cheeks as they ambled along, their conversation bound by periods of comfortable silence, against the beauty of the Lake, which Sahel could not see. Sahel could not see the beauty in herself; she considered herself ugly. She looked nothing like her mother except for her arched eyebrows, and the color and length of her hair. Sahel had felt dead alongside her mother. Lillian's vicious words had shot her into a muted oblivion where only work with clients brought her to life, offered the hope of light. And then Sahel had lost her sight.

She grew anxious as her thoughts wandered. *I need to move forward—either have the surgery, or learn to live independently as a person without sight.*

Reynard interrupted her reverie. "My client doesn't even know how her husband lost his sight."

Carl knew *how* but not *why* Sahel had lost hers. "How did you feel when listening to her? What was she like in session?"

"Striking."

A smile quirked upon Sahel's lips. "You're attracted to her?"

Reynard fell quiet, then commented, "She actually used

the word *striking* several times to describe the woman who intervened and stopped the woman with pink hair from cutting the man's throat."

"Tell me the story again." Reynard recounted his remembrance of what his client had told him.

"Besides reliving what happened in Nigeria," Sahel said, "what else affected her during the restaurant incident?"

"Believe it or not, the husband of the woman who intervened."

"Oh, the *striking* one?" she teased.

Again Reynard paused. After a moment, he spoke again, breaking the silence between them: "My client trained with Amos Morgan at an analytic institute in New York. I think she loves him. She loves her husband too. The sticking point appears to be that Amos can see her."

"But does *she* know that?"

"Does it matter?" Reynard was curt.

You'll meet her only when you can look into her eyes and tell me that she loves me as much as I love you.

❧

Sahel and Titus's mothers were Creole. Though unrelated, their relationship had gone beyond that which connected many siblings. Lillian was severely depressed when Cecile died. Sometimes she confined herself to her room. At other times, Lillian directed her anger at Sahel. She was also suspicious of Carl. She feared he might tarnish Sahel's reputation. He was not Creole.

Before Cecile Denning's death, Sahel, Titus, and Carl studied at Sahel's in her father's den. Sahel and Carl met in the library after Cecile's death. Sahel received the brunt of Lillian's rage when she got home.

Sahel was terrified at her mother's outbursts. Lillian often hit her. On one occasion, Lillian slapped Sahel, then clutched at her own chest and fell to the floor. Her first heart attack. Sahel called the paramedics.

❧

Reynard's voice cut through the dense forest of Sahel's thoughts as they continued along the lake's edge. "I don't understand how my client's husband has avoided telling her how he lost his sight. It makes no sense. She's an analyst. It's her job to probe."

"Maybe she doesn't want to know. She has her secret; he has his. It's what binds them."

"I never thought about it that way."

During the ride home, Sahel replayed all Reynard had said. Something was missing. Reynard was a good man, a precise psychiatrist and therapist. But something, some piece...

Reynard pulled into the driveway and helped her out of the car. He closed her door. "I never considered that secrets were an important part of maintaining a relationship—at least in *their* relationship." He then mused, "Perhaps I'm not the best person for her to be working with."

"Of course you are. Secrets are the most important piece of what we do. Whether we like it or not, we're keeping them—as long as it doesn't put our clients or anyone else in physical danger. Without doing this, they'd never feel safe enough to tell us what's frightening them. The key is to keep her talking."

Sahel flashed back to her accident. It had occurred in this very driveway. She had been searching the pavement for Titus's ring.

Reynard said, "You've given me a lot to think about."

"Anytime."

"Can I bank on that?"

"You have my number." As he started to walk her to the front door, his hand at her elbow, she extended her cane. "I can take it from here," she said, "As far as I can see—" She stopped, absorbed the irony of her words, and thanked Reynard for calling on her.

⁂

Two years earlier, Sahel had stood by her mother's bed. "I'm sorry," Lillian Ohin uttered, her heart fighting for each beat. "I was wrong. Please…" Weakened beyond words, she slipped the ring bearing an oval-shaped stone onto Sahel's finger and brought Sahel's and Titus's hands together. For the first time, Sahel felt loved by her mother.

Three hours later, Sahel opened the door of her psychotherapy office to Titus and Carl. Her mother was dead.

The accident had occurred five months after Lillian's death. Sahel and Titus were having an argument in the driveway of Sahel's childhood home.

"Our mothers were like sisters," Titus pleaded.

"I need time." Sahel couldn't set a wedding date.

"For what? To choose between me and Carl?" Sahel started away. Titus grabbed her arm. Again she pulled back her hand. Her fingers slipped through Titus's.

Upstairs in her old bedroom, Sahel discovered the engagement ring was missing from her finger. She raced down the stairs, out the door, and onto the driveway. She paid no attention to the fact that Titus had parked just in front of where she crouched. He only had one way out.

Sahel was on her knees, scouring the pavement like a child searching wildly for her mother in a dense forest of monsters and dragons when Titus put the car in reverse, proceeded to back out. The last thing she remembers are the tail lights blaring red, exhaust filling her nose. She fell to the driveway. All went black.

The ring symbolized everything to Sahel. He hadn't meant to hit her.

2:00 p.m.
Sahel stepped into the house. The voices from the living room grew louder. "Why didn't you tell me she was going out with Reynard Williams?" Titus was in guardian mode. He had arrived at home, and the housekeeper, Zelda, had stated that Sahel had gone out, but "not with Señor Pierson."

Titus had called Carl. Carl came over, and the argument ensued.

"Sahel's a grown woman. You can't keep her locked up."

"She's not a prisoner," Titus shouted.

"She is as long as you prevent her from having the surgery."

"I'm not stopping her from doing anything."

"Like hell you aren't. Every time it's mentioned, you run and get a second opinion—and tell her all the reasons she shouldn't have it."

"There's a fifty-percent chance she could die."

"And another fifty that she could live. With sight!"

The screaming match reminded Sahel of the fencing matches between Titus and Carl at Oakland Hills Catholic Prep, and then at Cal. Though always on the same team, they'd fenced with each other in practice to hone their skills.

"She's my wife," Titus said. Sahel closed the front door and moved toward the living room.

"Then you'd better get used to her blindness."

"If this is your way of trying to make me force her to have the surgery, then you've got another—"

"Sahel is blind. Without the surgery she has no hope of seeing again." Carl's words reached a crescendo. Sahel stopped outside the door.

"You can't have it both ways," Carl said. "She needs a seeing-eye dog or some type of aid for getting around. You're going to have to let her—"

"You're just angry that she chose me over you."

"That you married her won't give her sight."

"Shut up!" Titus's command rattled both old and newly risen ghosts. Two weeks after her accident, Sahel had wielded a knife in a fit of rage. Unable to get close to her, Titus had instructed Sahel's father to call Carl. Carl came, and while he spoke to her, Titus came from behind and wrestled the knife from her grasp.

Carl had called the paramedics to take Sahel to the

hospital, fearful that she might harm herself. Titus proposed again while awaiting their arrival. Sahel said yes.

Sahel now folded her cane and reentered her most painful memory.

※

Sahel was eleven. She lowered her hands into the water. A kaleidoscope of colors danced on the surface. Dirt lay underneath. She pushed her hands into the mud, felt it seep between her fingers. Titus's fingers followed in search of hers. Carl's came behind.

It was Rapture. Ascension.

Seconds later Titus pushed Carl's hands aside. "Move out of the way." He touched Sahel. Carl's fingers continued to intercede.

Caught in the wonder of the colors and mud, Sahel remained unconscious to the world of differences swirling about her. "I told you to get out of the way." Titus pulled Carl's hands from the bucket.

"Don't do that again." Carl's words broke the spell.

"Shhhhh." Sahel turned to them. "Momma's going to come outside and make you leave."

"No she won't," said Titus. "She'll just make you leave, Carl. My mother and Sahel's mother are friends. Mrs. Ohin doesn't like your mother. And she doesn't like you." Carl hit Titus and ran off. Titus rushed after him.

Worried that her mother had heard the argument, Sahel went into the house. She tiptoed into the living room and crouched beneath the windowsill, where she could hear Lillian and Cecile talking.

"They told me to leave and never come back when I said I was pregnant. I wanted to keep the baby," Lillian said.

An only child, the word "pregnant" piqued Sahel's curiosity. She inched upward and watched Lillian pour Cecile a glass of iced tea.

"They didn't like Essien," Lillian continued. "'He's African, and too dark,' my mother said. It didn't matter that he had graduated college or had been accepted to law school."

"I didn't know Essien was a lawyer." Cecile seemed genuinely surprised, and troubled.

"He never graduated," Lillian said. "Decided to get his PhD in economics and teach at that university over in the City instead of Cal." Lillian's words had been clear and abrupt—she was always critical of Sahel's father.

"He's a good man, Lillian. He loves Sahel."

"Sahel's not like you and me. She's dark."

"That doesn't matter these days." Sahel considered the color of her arms, ebony like her father's.

"Sahel is beautiful," said Cecile.

"You really think so?"

"Titus loves her. So do I. He would never let anyone hurt her. Ever." Sahel peered across the windowsill, and saw Cecile take her mother's hand. "You're like the sister I never had." Cecile's soft Alabama drawl sounded honest. "Ever since we moved to Oakland, you and Essien have been there for me and Howard, watching over us. Sahel is like my daughter. If anything ever happened to you, I'd be there for her." The glow of Cecile's smile spread across her face, fair and nearly white, like Lillian's.

Titus entered the living room. "The mud cakes are drying. Let's go get some ice cream." His face, fair with green undertones, was tanned from playing in the sun. Carl followed him in. Sahel jumped up, her heart racing.

"Why were you down on the floor like that?" Titus asked. Carl, with his quiet manner and dark skin, said nothing.

The screen door flew open and Lillian rushed through. "Haven't I told you about listening to adult conversations?" She grabbed Sahel.

"Go outside." Cecile opened the screen door and reached for Titus.

"But it was me and Carl that were arguing, not Sahel."

"Later." She motioned for Carl to go too.

⁂

The memory of placing her hand in the mud had absorbed Sahel entirely as she stood outside her living room door.

Titus's voice broke through, telling Carl to stay out of his and Sahel's marriage.

Sahel retreated into memories of more recent experiences. She had willed herself not to want Titus as she took each successive capsule. Loving Titus meant seeing her mother as a person.

Titus and Carl's voices grew louder. "She might have married you," Carl said, "but who walks with her by the Lake every Wednesday? Whose number does she dial in the middle of the night when you've fallen asleep poring over patient's charts?"

"If you're so fucking great then where were you when she took those pills and almost ended up a vegetable?"

"Trying to let you be her husband." Carl delivered his feint.

Sahel had hoped marrying Titus would kill her ambivalence. Saying the words "I do" with Carl looking on as best man had only made it worse. Her hand shook around the cane. She unfolded it and began to walk away.

Titus stormed out of the living room and into the foyer. Sahel was moving toward the stairs when he rushed to her. Startled, she steadied herself and turned toward him. "I consulted with Reynard Williams about one of his clients."

"For two hours?" Titus's voice softened as he placed his hands upon her shoulders. "You could have talked with him here."

"I suggested that we walk by the Lake." Titus's hand slid down her arm. She felt him about to take her cane. Carl, now behind her, squeezed her shoulder.

Bewilderment took over. Sahel shrugged off their hands, felt her way to the stairs, and sat down. Titus again took hold of her hand. "I need my cane!" She pulled back. After folding her cane, she patted the spaces on her left and right, indicating for Titus and Carl to sit. "I need you. *Both* of you."

Titus and Carl hung their heads. Sahel reached out for Titus, felt him interweave his fingers with hers. She felt Carl's hand doing the same with her left hand.

Her tears, the first in months, rekindled the image of red, yellow, and green light radiating through the water on the day she, Carl, and Titus had mixed mud cakes.

"I don't know if or when I'm going to have the surgery," she said to Titus. "Until then, I'm going to use my cane." Carl cradled her hand with both of his. She turned to him grateful that he had held her silence, let her be the one, like Reynard's client to disclose it. "Thank you."

Sahel explained. "All my life, I felt Momma hated me." Carl and Titus had witnessed Lillian's wrath toward Sahel. Carl had also heard Lillian's secret. "I didn't think she wanted me," Sahel continued. "Then, twenty years later, she apologized and put her ring on my finger."

Carl had stood beside Essien and witnessed Lillian telling Sahel and Titus how much she and Cecile had wanted them to marry.

Sahel and Titus are our only hope of salvation.

"When I saw the ring wasn't on my finger, all I could think of was—I just wanted it back. This was never Titus's fault."

Reynard's words floated through her mind. *My client said learning why her husband is blind might make her stop loving him.*

Sahel turned to Carl again. "I should have told you why the ring was so important. It's just that…" Sahel sobbed. "I wish this had never hap—"

"You're my friend," Carl assured her as he unfolded her cane and placed it in her hand. Sahel felt herself come to life.

5:00 p.m.
Titus rested his hands upon the nape of Sahel's neck. They were in the seclusion of their bedroom. "You look like my mother," she said.

"Is that so bad?"

"I'm dark…"

"I felt you leaving me this afternoon, when I was arguing with Carl." Titus kissed the back of her head as he did every morning.

"I need you, Titus. Let me love you. All I have from my childhood are memories of our fingers touching in the sand."

Warmth traveled down Sahel's spine and radiated throughout her body as he touched her. He said, "My mother thought you were beautiful. She loved you. So do I.

"When Zelda said you had gone out, and without Carl, I—" Titus retrieved Sahel's cane from the bed and opened it. He placed it upon her palm. "I came home early—was thinking perhaps that we could walk the…"

An image broke the surface of her memory— red fading to black, and then her and Titus's hands coming together underneath the water and sand. The ambivalence that held Sahel hostage submerged along with sad memories of Lillian.

Titus's lanky eleven-year-old body had moved slowly and without aim at the airport. Defeat stung his eyes, which were red and swollen. He had returned to Oakland two years after his parents' deaths.

Another image emerged of the mud, and how the water above cast a rainbow on their hands below—Titus and Sahel's hands.

"You're all I've ever wanted," Titus murmured now, as he held her in their bedroom.

Sahel reached up to touch his throat. The throb of his jugular pulsated in sync with hers.

"Can we go to the Lake, Sahel?"

Sahel's fingers stroked his cheek, wiped his unseen tears. "Yes."

The Object of Compassion

Reynard Williams placed the envelope inside the drawer, closed and relocked it. He sat in the chair in his study and stared at the Buddha in the garden beyond the window. Water flowed from the icon's upturned palms. Two arc-shaped streams descended into the pool below.

Reynard hadn't felt this low since his mother had undergone her first schizophrenic break. He had been fifteen, his four older sisters away at college. Reynard's father, an executive for American Express, had continued traveling during the week. The minister's wife had seen to Reynard's mother during the day; Reynard was her guardian at night.

Reynard breathed in and sighed. Tomorrow he would learn whether the doctors had extracted enough sperm from his testicles to impregnate his wife Aaron.

Tears of frustration burned from behind his eyelids. First they had learned that Aaron hadn't been ovulating. After the fertility specialist extracted some of Aaron's eggs, he then found that Reynard had a low sperm count. In the middle of it all, Reynard lost his ability to mount an erection.

Most men experiencing erectile dysfunction could contribute sperm with manual stimulation. Reynard could not. He received a prescription of Viagra from the urologist and then gave a sample. Examination of his semen revealed less than half the normal amount of sperm.

"We'll need a concentrated sample for Aaron's insemination," the specialist had said over the phone.

"Next you'll tell me they don't work."

"Don't worry Reynard—they're viable—just like Aaron's eggs. We just need more of them." The specialist, a golfing buddy of Reynard's, understood the sensitive nature of the matter. "Don't beat yourself up. You and Aaron have been through a lot. Hang in there."

Reynard and Aaron had endured much, before and after they met.

⁂

The paramedics had delivered Aaron to the emergency room of Manhattan General twelve years ago. Dirty and unkempt, she had been wearing a fur coat. Her hair was matted; she was nearly catatonic. Both wrists had been slit open by a razor—difficult to achieve even by the most suicidal. Reynard was chief psychiatry resident.

While nurses gave the unidentified female a Betadine wash, Reynard examined her coat for clues to her identity. The initials A.B.M. were embroidered underneath the back collar. A card in the right-hand pocket bore the name of Aaron's father, a trustee and former president of the First African American Bank in Baltimore. The pocket also contained a one-and-a-half-carat diamond ring.

Aaron awoke two days later. Her parents had not revealed her husband Kevin's name or contact information, and she refused to allow Reynard to contact him. She told him that her three-year-old son had died of leukemia in November. It was then February.

"What of your husband?" Reynard asked.

"What of him?" Aaron's brown eyes held a blankness resembling that of Reynard's mother's, weeks after her first psychotic break.

"I'm sure he's worried about you."

"I doubt that." Aaron lowered her head. "Kevin's a busy man. With me out of his life, he's free to get on with things— get on with life."

Aaron was Reynard's psychiatry patient. He needed to

get to the root of her problem, to figure out what about her son's death had caused her to try to end her own life. But Aaron wouldn't talk about why her parents refused to give Kevin's address to Reynard. Aaron did say Kevin wasn't present at the time of their son's death.

"Where was he?"

"At work."

According to Aaron, Kevin Blackwell was a new partner at one of Manhattan's most lucrative banks. He had been carrying out a merger when their son died. On arriving at the hospital, he had pried Aaron's fingers from their son Layson's, whose body lay cooling in her lap. He had taken her home, and they had buried Layson the next day. Kevin had gone to work the day after.

Reynard didn't believe Aaron's story at first; it sounded too harsh. He called Roosevelt Hospital and spoke with the head nurse on the oncology floor.

"It was sad," the nurse said. "Mrs. Blackwell stayed here night and day. Always beside Layson's bed."

"And where was Mr. Blackwell?"

"Where he always was—at work." The nurse confirmed what Aaron had said.

"One of our nurses, Sandy, called his office just after Dr. Granville pronounced the boy dead. That was noon. Mr. Blackwell's secretary said he was in a meeting. When Sandy told her that his son had died, the secretary put her on hold. A couple of seconds later, she came back and said that Mr. Blackwell would be there as soon as possible." The nurse sighed. "We didn't know what to do. Mrs. Blackwell was in no shape to go home. Dr. Granville told us to let her stay with Layson until Mr. Blackwell came. He arrived at five o'clock sharp."

Reynard hung up the phone, unable to fathom Kevin Blackwell's actions. Reynard had seen a fair number of clients during his residency—many of them men, angry and hurting. *But how could Aaron's husband be so cold?*

Then, as now, Reynard sat at the desk in his on-call room. He could only think of one answer.

Kevin Blackwell is like my father.

Reynard had traveled to the Himalayas and studied Tibetan Buddhism with a lama for one year before entering his psychiatry residency. Through meditation, he tried to quell his anger toward his father. Reynard's father, Robert Williams, thought psychiatry a waste of Reynard's skill and talent. "Shrinks don't make any money," Robert had said.

These days, the insurance companies with whom Reynard contracted were urging him to administer more medication, to meet with his patients only once a month, as opposed to each week, to monitor their progress. But Reynard liked providing a space for his patients to discuss their lives and hear their own voices. He liked giving them what he had given his mother, seeing them smile, hearing them say thank you.

As a child, Reynard had always known great joy on the good days, such as when Patricia Williams had driven him to Cub Scout meetings. When tucking him into bed, she'd always said, "My Rennie." Then, before turning off the lamp, she would add, "As long as the sun rises and sets, you'll be my son. Forever and a day." She had then kissed his cheek, and left.

Years later and in the wilds of schizophrenia, she had seldom cried. The minister's wife, who lived next door, saw to Reynard's mother during the day. She fed and dressed Patricia for bed in the early evening, and then left her in Reynard's care for the night.

Reynard was a responsible child. He could handle it, Robert Williams had concluded, and Reynard had to because Robert needed to work to provide for his family. But even Reynard didn't hold the answers to Patricia Williams's questions. "Where's your father, Rennie? Doesn't he love us anymore?"

"He does." Reynard had whispered, as he kissed the tear

on her cheek. He had pondered the same question himself.

"This is all my fault."

"No, ma'am." It had become difficult for him to call her "Momma." The mental illness had imprisoned both mother and son.

* The silence and loneliness following those occasions when he had to urge his mother, "Go back to sleep," came to life again when he learned that he didn't carry enough sperm to impregnate Aaron without medical intervention. Medicine hadn't helped Reynard's mother. Neither had it assisted him with his impotence. He feared it would not help now.

It was these memories that Aaron's entry into Reynard's life twelve years ago had enlivened to the point of cracking. His long-held frustration had poured forth a week after her admission to the hospital. The social worker overseeing Aaron's care had approached Reynard. "Dr. Williams, I see that you're carrying out sessions with Mrs. Blackwell in her room." Anna Daniels, the fifty-four-year old social worker with thirty years of experience, forbid residents to conduct psychiatric sessions in the patient's room unless physical injury prevented them from being transported to the psychiatrist or resident's office.

"I don't want patients getting the wrong impression," she would say, particularly if the patient was a woman and the psychiatrist a man. "Do you know what I mean, Dr. Williams?" Daniels reminded Reynard of her admonishment to all psychiatry residents at the outset of their training. Reynard was then chief resident three months from completing his training.

"She's *my* patient," he said. "And I'll see her where she's most comfortable."

"Nurses are tending her wrists, Dr. Williams," the social worker went on. "As far as I can see—"

"But you can't see! And I'm her psychiatrist."

"I know you want her off the floor." Daniels pushed on.

"She has no insurance."

"You don't know what she has."

"To this date we have no identification on this—on your patient, who calls herself Aaron Blackwell. And even that is suspicious."

Reynard had frowned.

"Aaron is a male name, you know," Daniels added with a smug look on her face.

Reynard had not considered the abstraction. It was indeed strange. But he had been taken with Aaron's frailty, her suffering, his need to heal and fix.

"She's been here one week," Daniels said as she opened Aaron's chart, "And as far as I can see—"

"Like I said, you can't see a damn thing." Reynard snatched the manila folder from the woman with white hair and piercing hazel eyes. He ripped it to shreds. "Leave. Her. Alone." The eyes of the social worker grew big in the face of his temper. "She's my patient. I won't have you messing with her." Reynard stormed off.

Later that day, in the office of the attending psychiatrist under whom he had worked most of his residency, Reynard explored his earlier behavior.

"She's married but won't talk with her husband." Reynard said of Aaron. "Her parents haven't said they'd contact him either, but..." His voice trailed off. His attention wandered to the *Annals of Psychiatry* lining the shelves behind Dr. Ambrose's desk.

The gray-haired psychiatrist who had emigrated from Russia at the age of nine followed Reynard's gaze toward the shelves behind him. "Those can't help you; the answer is within your heart." He glanced back at Reynard. A practicing Buddhist, Ambrose had directed Reynard to Lama Pol in the Himalayas after accepting Reynard into the psychiatry program.

"You're in love." The psychiatrist knew of Reynard's run-in with the social worker long before Reynard confessed. He smiled.

Reynard lowered his head. "I know I haven't made enough of an effort to find her husband. Neither have I pushed Aaron's parents to tell me why they and she are avoiding him. It's just that—"

"She makes you think of your mother." Ambrose also knew Reynard's story. That's why he'd counseled him to spend a year in the Himalayas.

"She's like no other client. I can't clear my thoughts of her the way I do with other patients." Reynard had already begun thinking of what psychiatric resident he might transfer Aaron to, which was why he'd asked to see Ambrose. Clearly Reynard had taken out his anger upon the social worker.

"There are many fine residents here. I'll leave it to you to decide," Ambrose said. "But before you do any of that, have you considered who your father is in this?"

Reynard was silent.

"Hmm…I see from your notes that Mrs. Blackwell has stated she doesn't want to see her husband, says her marriage is over. They've experienced the loss of a child." Ambrose glanced up from his reading, "Are they divorced?"

Reynard had never asked.

"And if so, who initiated it?"

On leaving Ambrose's office Reynard transferred Aaron's care to a fellow resident who would then find her an appropriate psychiatrist. That was procedure.

Later he went to Aaron's room. Finding her gone, he inquired at the nurses' station if Aaron was with her new psychiatrist.

"No, Dr. Williams," the nurse said. "Mrs. Daniels discharged her."

Paramedics returned two nights later with Aaron on a gurney. This time she had taken an overdose of sleeping pills. Emergency room doctors revived her. Daniels was summarily fired, and Dr. Ambrose took on Aaron's case.

Nine months later, with all the divorce papers signed and

Aaron free from a husband Reynard knew little about, he married her.

Reynard's father called hours before Reynard wed Aaron.

"She's getting combative, hasn't recognized me for months." Robert Williams said, as if discussing an account he wanted to close out.

"She gets that way sometimes. We've talked about this." Reynard's tone was stern.

"I live with the woman 24/7," the elder Williams said. "It's impossible to keep her safe."

"You're tired. You need someone to come in and help."

"And what are they going to do, laugh at her? She's a mess, and the place is a pigsty; the woman you knew as your mother is gone, Reynard. That's why I'm—"

"I lived with her for four years."

"She's my wife."

"I don't want my mother in a mental institution."

"Look, son, I'm not divorcing her. I'm just trying to take care of myself so I can be here to see to her."

"And how do you plan on doing that with her in some—"

"The internist and psychiatrist are in agreement."

"They're quacks; I know a—"

"It's done. I put your mother there last night."

Reynard resented his father's having acted before calling him. It was reminiscent of how Robert Williams had moved up the professional ladder.

"It's what she and *I* need. Now you need to get married."

Reynard laid down the phone. He said nothing to Aaron.

During the ceremony, she pledged to stand beside him forever. "You saved my life." Her brown eyes glistened with tears. "Each day I give honor to the fact that there are no coincidences." She reached up and kissed him. Reynard vowed to love her until death, in sickness and in health, wealth and poverty, for all that was good, and despite all challenges. He never considered he might be one of those challenges.

The door to Reynard's study opened, and Aaron appeared. "Why didn't you wake me?"

"You need your rest." Aaron was exhausted from all the poking and prodding to isolate the reason she wasn't conceiving. Reynard urged her to take afternoon naps.

"What about you?" She knelt down before him.

"I'm fine."

"What does Ansak say?"

Reynard routinely met with Ansak Rinpoche who ran the Berkeley temple. A convert to Tibetan Buddhism, Aaron also met with the Rinpoche.

"I took the medication." He glanced back at the locked drawer.

"But what does Ansak suggest?"

Green Tara. Ansak's words floated on Reynard's consciousness. *You need to meditate on Green Tara.* A manifestation of Quan Yen, Green Tara was the goddess of active compassion.

Reynard's heart had melted on that cold night in February, when he saw Aaron lying on the gurney in the emergency room. She had been staring into space. It was Valentine's Day.

Now, under the watchful eyes of the Buddha outside their window, he turned over Aaron's wrists, caressing their thick scars, evidence of the surgeon's repair.

"How can you still love him—Kevin?"

"Where'd that come from?"

He shook his head. "But you do."

Aaron's parents had visited two weeks ago. Aaron's mother, Clancy, no fan of Kevin, had reiterated her feelings about Aaron's ex-husband. "He's the bad seed—brought so much pain to this family. I hope never to see him again. God help anyone who's stupid enough to marry him now." Clancy saw Reynard as Aaron's savior.

Aaron and her father continued eating their asparagus.

Reynard sliced his trout with the precision of a surgeon, despite its softness.

Clancy continued her treatise throughout the meal. "Here you are, your only child dead. And now with Reynard, who loves you, you're unable to conceive another. It's unfair, terribly unfair."

"Kevin didn't cause our problems." Aaron said.

"Like hell he didn't!"

"Now, Clancy." Aaron's father, Theodore, moved to quiet his wife. Clancy waved him away. Reynard placed another slice of trout into his mouth. Clancy's words gave him solace. Both he and Clancy loved Aaron. But Clancy didn't know of Reynard's low sperm count.

Aaron then said, "Kevin was doing the best he could. We were both hurting."

"How can you say that?" Clancy frowned.

"Perhaps if you'd not judged him so much from the beginning—"

Bitterness overcame Reynard, almost forcing him to spit out his food. There was forgiveness, and there was compassion. But this was ludicrous.

Clancy forged on. "I'm just saying, Aaron—"

"That's enough!" Aaron stood, surprising Clancy and her father, but no one more so than Reynard. Aaron's brown eyes were soft like his mother's, but lacked the frail yearning that had overtaken Patricia's. They glistened with strength.

⁂

The two streams of water rising from the Buddha's palms seemed almost invisible against the late-afternoon light.

Reynard glanced back at the locked drawer. Ten days remained for him to respond to the insurance company's demand couched in a request.

"Do you love Kevin more than you love me?" he quietly asked.

"Of course not."

"I want to know."

"That's like wanting to know if I like myself more the way I am now than the way I was twelve years ago."

"Do you?"

"I am who I am because of what we—Kevin and I—went through." Aaron hit her chest. "Without him, I don't know if I'd be able to appreciate and love you."

An adept psychiatrist, Reynard had presented Aaron a riddle to which only he held the answer. "Aren't you angry at him?"

"What good would that do?"

"Were you angry at him when Layson was dying?"

"Kevin was hurting—"

"You always do that—defend him!" Reynard held his breath for a moment. "You donated so much marrow. Your blood counts dropped to a dangerous level."

"Kevin's blood type didn't match Layson's."

"He should have been with you."

"Would that have saved Layson?" Aaron said softly.

Reynard was angry at Kevin, and at the healing Aaron had accomplished. And he was still angry with his father. As with the social worker twelve years earlier, Reynard now extended those feelings to Kevin Blackwell.

Reynard routinely prescribed medication for his patients, but he also believed true healing resulted from attending to both the physical and the psychological. Reynard felt absent from Aaron—like he had become his father, home on weekends and often absent both in spirit and physical presence from those who loved him.

Reynard still could not mount an erection. Aaron was still the beautiful woman he had married twelve years ago in the backyard of her parents' Baltimore home, but he had lost his sexual desire. Reynard felt he had given Aaron no more than Kevin Blackwell, possibly not even as much.

Aaron shook him gently. "I love you. For better and for worse, in sickness and in health, and through all the crazy things life throws our way. *I love you.*"

Reynard wanted to believe her, but felt he was disappointing her as a husband and a lover. "I want you to have a child." He struggled to say the words.

The young man whose mother's mental illness had swallowed her whole still yearned to make her better, still wanted his mother to recognize and love him.

But Reynard had been the one who stayed with his mother, like he had stayed with Aaron and helped her back to life at the end of her marriage with Kevin. Reynard wanted to be the perfect man for Aaron, give her all he felt she didn't get from Kevin, the hard worker, the great provider. Like his father. Reynard was tired of competing with his father.

Aaron studied him intently. She knew of Reynard's frustration with his father. "You need to let go of your anger. Your father was just doing the best he could."

"Oh, like Kevin?" he demanded.

"Like me and you," she said as she touched his chest, then took him into her arms. In the deepest moments of sadness, Reynard felt himself crying for Layson, a little boy now deceased, one whom Reynard had never met. At times he dreamed of Layson, held in purgatory and longing for Aaron and him, not Kevin.

A slow burn heated his blood, then dissipated as they held each other. Reynard wanted to desire Aaron, to feel the attraction and power of making love to his wife as he had in the past. He pulled away from her embrace and turned back to the garden. Water still flowed from the Buddha's palms amid last flickers of daylight. Night had descended.

⁂

Reynard's first two clients left messages saying they couldn't make their appointments. In the interim and throughout the session with his third client—a married man having an affair—he ruminated upon Aaron's inability to see past his frustration to his hurt, and his inability to explain it.

The Object of Compassion

Reynard was headed out the back of the building when he chanced upon Ramona Bennett. At sixty-one, Ramona was interning as a marriage and family therapist under one of the psychiatrists down the hall from Reynard's office. In a month, she would sit for her oral exam toward licensure.

"Ramona." He rushed to help her load the box of charts into her car.

"Thank you." She smiled. "I saw your car when I came in this morning to study. Figured you had an early patient."

"So much for coming in at seven-thirty. The first two cancelled. And, well, the third..." Reynard extended his hand to her.

Ramona pulled Reynard into a hug and kissed his cheek. "I can do that since you told me I'm older than your mother." He forced a smile as she continued, "Have you had lunch? But then, you're probably headed for the temple." Reynard usually meditated during his lunch hour.

"They're cleaning the carpets."

"Well, Calvin's meeting with Demetrius, so I was going to grab a sandwich." Demetrius Olay was one of Ramona and Calvin Bennett's three sons-in-law. "Would you like to join me?" She closed and locked the car door. "We haven't talked for a while."

Ramona had often lauded Reynard's commitment to salvage and preserve his own soul, unlike so many in their profession. In her estimation, "That year you spent in the Himalayas will deliver dividends long into your future and lifetimes to come."

Reynard turned back to Ramona, the woman, an example of what his mother might have become had the schizophrenia not swept her away. "I'd like that." His soul settled onto the tarmac of compassion that Ramona exuded to all with whom she came in contact.

"Then I suppose we have a date." She entwined her arm with his.

 ✹ Ramona opened her napkin and spread her arms

akimbo on the table covered in white linen. She and Reynard sat under a red umbrella, which shaded their table at an open-air restaurant on Berkeley's Fourth Street.

"How's Aaron holding up?"

"We're getting ready to undergo insemination. It seems that she hasn't been ovulating."

"Do they know how long or why?"

"No." Reynard shook his head. "I'm sure it has to do with the stress she was under when Layson died."

"But that was twelve years ago." Ramona frowned.

Ramona had three children and three grandchildren. She was easy to talk to. Reynard had spoken to her previously about Aaron's first marriage, saying nothing of his resentment toward Kevin, and little of his mother, except, "She lives in a home—early dementia."

The autumn sun filling the parking lot reminded Reynard of his mother taking him to buy school supplies each September back in Mt. Kisco, New York. "My mother was diagnosed with schizophrenia when I was thirteen," he said now. Ramona smiled. Reynard found himself doing the same, puzzled as he was by her response.

"We're so funny, us black people." The sixty-one-year-old woman wearing pearls and a fuchsia dress gave a hearty giggle, and then with motherly softness, "I thought so."

"How? What did I say?"

"It was what you didn't."

Reynard pocketed his hands, now aware of that which he had been unconscious.

He told Ramona about life as an adolescent with his mother during the weeks while his father was on the road. "It was hard. My sisters were away at college and grad school. Dad seemed oblivious. And Momma ... " He turned to the parking lot. The sun was at its zenith. He hadn't said the word, "Momma" in over a decade. His eyes welled.

"Momma was a bright and beautiful woman before everything went haywire. She helped me with my homework, attended PTA meetings, baked brownies for my Cub Scout troop ... " Reynard stared at the gold band on his left finger. "And then there's Aaron's first husband. I can't seem to get him out of my mind."

Ramona rolled with the change in conversational direction. "Have you met him?"

"No. And quite frankly, I don't want to."

"You can't tell me that all the hours you've spent meditating haven't done something." Ramona smiled. "Marriage requires a lot from us," she continued. "It's an evolutionary process—some say a spiritual path unto its own."

"Any words of wisdom?"

"You have to hang in there."

⁂

Robert Williams had been arranging flowers in a vase on the nightstand the day that Reynard first knocked on the door to his mother's room at the convalescent home. He had turned from the nightstand—a gift purchased for her on a business trip to Bangkok—and rushed to greet his son and new daughter-in-law.

Reynard shook his father's hand, and after introducing him to Aaron, went to his mother. He knelt before the woman whose every movement he had worshipped as a child. She was staring at the television.

"Hi, Momma." Reynard touched her hand. "I completed my residency. Got married."

Reynard motioned for Aaron, and in that instant, missed the darkness that had slid over his mother's eyes. He turned back to her. "We're headed for California, but I wanted you to meet her. Momma, this is Aaron."

Reynard's mother had peered up at Aaron. "You're a lovely girl." Then to Reynard, "Have you seen my son? She would be perfect for him."

Reynard hadn't told Aaron about his mother until days before the wedding, when he had accepted the fact that his mother would be unable to attend the ceremony.

"It's me, Reynard." He tried to reclaim his mother's memory and his place in her life.

"You're not my son," Patricia Williams said, becoming agitated. "Reynard would never go away and leave me." As quickly as it had flared, her anxiety passed. A smile crossed her lips, then widened. "My son is back home keeping everything together for when I return."

⁂

Reynard didn't realize he had bent the fork until Ramona pried it from his fingers. She placed the maimed object upon her napkin and folded the white layers around it.

"Anger is one of the most powerful tools we possess. It's not a nice emotion. Nor is it pretty. But anger is loyal."

The mother of three daughters and wife of a heart surgeon, Ramona glanced toward the parking lot as she said, "Thirty-five years ago, I walked in on Calvin making love to his secretary. They were in the bedroom of a condo we own over in Alameda. I became suspicious when Calvin told the real estate agent he had no plans for renting it out; I had a key made before we signed the closing papers."

"Calvin was just in practice, and doing well. His senior partner, Martin Tolman, had been nothing like Calvin is with Titus now." Ramona sighed. "Calvin had to do it all by himself." Her lips shifted into a bittersweet smile. "I go there, to the condo, to study for my licensure exam, sleep in the bed when I'm too tired to drive home. I refused to let Calvin sell it."

The taste of bile inched up Reynard's throat as he commented, "Everything is as it was."

Ramona then said, "Lilith is having an affair with Demetrius's agent; I'm certain of it." Lilith, her middle daughter, was a budding artist in Los Angeles. She was married to Demetrius Olay, a professional basketball player.

Ramona brought her hands together and interwove her

fingers. "I need to forgive Calvin," she said, looking directly at Reynard. He forced himself to meet her gaze.

The waiter delivered their entrees and left. Ramona picked up her fork and knife as she explained her situation from years earlier. "Elena, the secretary, was like family. We lunched every Saturday. Her son, Okai, played with Zena, our oldest."

"Is her son ... ?"

"No, no." Ramona waved her palm and smiled, leaving Reynard again to contemplate her quiet amusement. She said, "Elena divorced her husband six months before Calvin partnered with Tolman. Calvin had wanted me to work in his office like Tolman's wife had done during the early years of his practice. I answered by hiring Elena." Ramona's eyes faded into a past Reynard sensed she kept close.

"I'd been taking care of my father, the Baptist minister, since I was eight. That was the year I returned home from school one day and Daddy said, 'Momma died.' Of course, with no funeral, I'd always wondered. Then there were the whispers."

Ramona settled her gaze back upon the parking lot and was quiet for some time. "Daddy died two months after Calvin and I moved here from Atlanta. I'd just hired Elena. I arrived for the funeral at my home in North Carolina with Calvin and Zena to find my mother living in Daddy's house."

"For nearly twenty years, she had lived one county over with a white man. State law wouldn't allow them to marry. Momma had refused to move away. She returned home when Daddy suffered his stroke. The white man was dead. He had left her fairly well off." Ramona ran her fingertip along the edge of her water glass.

"I was furious that Momma hadn't called me until *after* Daddy died. I came back here never having spoken to her. I didn't know it at the time, but I'd been carrying Lilith. I caught Calvin with Elena seven months later." It took all

Reynard's will to contain a surge of sadness and fury.

"Anger is a powerful tool. It has to be directed at the right thing, and that's never the ones we love—or worse, ourselves."

"I hated my mother for leaving us." Ramona placed her palms upon his, which had curled into fists. "I hated my father for letting her take care of him instead of me."

"Would you have gone, had she called?" Reynard asked.

"Yes. But Calvin needed me." Ramona leaned forward. "Calvin is pompous and self-absorbed. He can be downright rude at times. He's also a wonderful and loving father and grandfather. He's an excellent cardiac surgeon. Calvin treats Titus like the son we never had—supports him and Sahel through all their trials."

"But does he love you?"

"As much as I've allowed him to."

Reynard reconsidered Lilith's extramarital dalliances, this time not in the light of her father's adulterous foibles, but her mother's anger.

"As a child," she continued, "I'd always known Daddy had been lying about Momma's death. I hated them both for keeping themselves to each other."

Reynard removed his shoes and entered the main meditation hall of the temple. He had come last Friday and found the icon of Green Tara occupying the place where the Buddha normally sat. Artisans had been refurbishing the ten-foot bronze statue of the Enlightened One, so Reynard left.

Five days passed. He had refused to sit before the deity manifesting the essence of compassion. He was unable to focus upon his breathing and couldn't meditate.

Reynard had lied to Ramona about his reason for not going to the temple. Hearing her truth had drawn him to his. He lowered himself onto the cushion, and crossed his legs.

Anger is a loyal and good friend, but not when we direct it toward the ones we love—or ourselves.

He closed his eyes. The landscape of a park emerged upon his consciousness. A smiling boy sat upon a swing. His mother pushed him higher and higher, their ecstasy climbing with each push.

Reynard was dreaming with purpose and meaning— what Lama Pol had urged him to do upon returning from his year at the abbey near the base of the Himalayas.

Reynard inhaled and then centered his breath and thoughts upon Green Tara. The woman pushing the gleeful boy was Aaron.

As Reynard opened the gate and started toward them, a man approached Aaron, kissed her cheek. He lifted the boy from the swing, tousled his hair.

Kevin. Tears fell—each drop containing Reynard's vision. Aaron stood before him, Kevin beside her, the little boy between them.

Aaron directed the little boy to Reynard, who crouched down to receive him. *Layson.* He placed his arms around Reynard's neck and kissed his cheek. Reynard embraced the child whose heart beat against his.

The boy stepped back, and Reynard let go. Aaron and the man were no more. The boy too, was gone. Robert and Patricia Williams stood in their places, holding hands, and smiling. A green light hung about them.

Embrace your anger. Take it in.

Reynard moved toward his parents, who opened their arms to him. The green aura encompassed him. As sobs wracked his body, tears of anger mellowed into compassion.

A hand landed gently upon Reynard's shoulder. He turned, opened his eyes, and looked up. A four-foot man swathed in orange and with a shaved head smiled upon Reynard.

"I heard my son crying, and so I came," Lama Pol said.

The keeper of the temple, Ansak Rinpoche, had just driven the Tibetan monk from the airport. Reynard stood and embraced the man whose words had brought him freedom from his own limited vision.

Minutes later, having tea in the Rinpoche's quarters, he told the monk of his dream, or rather, waking vision. "I saw them, all of them," Reynard said. "Aaron, Kevin... and Layson. Aaron was pushing him in a swing. Kevin came. He kissed her and then swung Layson into his arms. I felt safe and loved. I cried," he said, his voice full of wonder. He looked to Lama Pol. "Then they were standing above me—my parents. I felt warm inside." Reynard said as he described their faces. "They were glowing green."

"They bore compassion, my son." The sixty-six-year-old monk, his orange robe appearing almost luminous, released a laugh. "Green Tara has visited her goodness upon you!" Lama Pol slapped his knee. "You have traveled to the heart of your pain, found the source of your frustration, made it the object of your compassion." He reached over and touched Reynard's chest. A green halo filled the room. Warmth spread throughout Reynard's body and filled his heart. Again he felt himself uplifted.

***

Reynard entered the kitchen and walked directly to his wife's side. She slid the stew into the oven, closed its door, and turned to him.

"You were right." He took her hands. "I needed to forgive my father."

"Have you?"

Reynard envisioned his parents and Lama Pol. The green light that had encompassed them and filled the room where he sat with Lama Pol now encircled him and Aaron.

Aaron. Strong in kindness. Reynard loved her for that. He stretched his fingers into the green mist and reached for his wife.

Compassion washed over them.

Reynard grew firm.

The Bridge

Michael Banks looked at his wife Rachel standing between her bridesmaids, and prepared himself to renew his wedding vows. Rachel's caramel face and brown eyes glowed against mid-morning sunlight radiating through the top pane of the stained glass windows bearing the image of Christ's Ascension. A smaller panel beside it held an image of Mary's Assumption.

Michael was an engineer who designed and oversaw the construction and refurbishing of bridges. Thirteen months ago he had fallen from the Richmond Bridge. Now, he struggled to remember the idiosyncrasies binding them, and ultimately why Rachel had married him the first time. Michael had no memory of their life together. He longed to know what sustained Rachel's undaunted patience as he attempted first to learn to walk, then to carry out simple tasks, and now tried to regain his memory.

Michael felt a hand upon his shoulder. He turned to find his best man, Greg, smiling. "So it's the big day—again," Greg said. "You were a box of jitters the first time you and Rachel tied the knot." Greg's smile widened above his neatly trimmed goatee. He straightened the white rose in the lapel of Michael's black tuxedo.

"Not this time." Michael turned back toward Rachel, who stood across the narthex. "I've got years with her under my belt."

Greg patted Michael's shoulder. "Rachel's a good person. The two of you are on the road all us marrieds are trying to get down." As a divorce attorney, Greg had seen his share of failed marriages. He clasped Michael in a congratulatory embrace.

Michael felt Greg's heart pounding against his chest. A strange awe came over him. The purple, red, and blue lights reflecting the glow of Christ's face enveloped Rachel and her bridesmaids.

Across the room, Rachel laughed. A horrible pain raced from the crown of Michael's head to the soles of his feet. Unaware of his agony, she broadened her smile. The pain in Michael's temples escalated. He slumped toward the floor.

"What's happening?" Michael heard the concern in Greg's voice as he eased him down.

Guests filing into the narthex became a blur, as did the priest now speaking with Rachel. Father Mitchell, who'd given Michael last rites after the fall from the bridge, took Rachel's hand between his, and in parental fashion, kissed her forehead.

A good man. Father Mitchell had prayed unceasingly with Rachel during the first forty-eight hours after Michael's fall.

I can't lose her, not again—not this time. The words fixed themselves in Michael's mind as they had a year ago. Michael looked to Greg and wished he could reach Rachel and pull her near him. The image of Christ ascending enlarged, obliterating that of Mary's journey into Heaven. Michael slipped into a semiconscious state.

A scene formed between his drifting thoughts. The joy of the narthex was gone. Michael and Rachel were standing in the kitchen.

"I need you. Can't you see that?" Rachel hit her chest.

The slivered memory expanded. Michael saw himself walking toward her. "It's my job."

"No! Building bridges is your obsession!" Frustration clouded Rachel's face. Again, Michael tried approaching her. She pushed him away. "How are we to have a family with you out there every day on those bridges? I won't go on like this."

"And what other line of work do you suggest I take up?" Michael had designed, constructed, and repaired bridges for over a decade. As a child, he had studied pictures of the Golden Gate, Richmond, and San Mateo bridges, along with the ancient ones. At thirty-six, bridges had become his life. Secretly, he liked inspecting the handiwork of his men. Hanging several feet under a bridge, held by a harness attached to a pulley, was ecstasy. The sky above, the wide expanse of the Pacific below—it was the greatest freedom.

Michael knew that what stood between people so often bound them. He reached for Rachel, but again she pushed him away. "Let the workers put the screws in. You're the brains on these projects. It's your plans they follow."

"I have to be there to see that it's done right."

"That's bull! You want to control everything!" Rachel was irate.

"You're trying to control me."

"I know they offered you that position in Sacramento. You want your track record spotless so that no one can come back and blame that black engineer for his shoddy work on whatever bridge." She waved her hand dismissively. Michael was a perfectionist. "We have a marriage, Michael. That's two people." She held up her fingers. "Two."

"I love you, Rachel. But I won't quit."

Rachel turned to the wall. Her hand was upon her hip. That's when Michael noticed—no wedding band.

⚜

The vision ended abruptly, and Michael lay on the floor in the narthex of St. Maria's. He tried to pray as he had during the fall. The multicolored light filling the stained glass window formed a thick halo around Rachel, who knelt beside him. Her full lips no longer held the ebullience from moments earlier, nor the anger and strife from the torn pieces of his memory. "Michael, what's wrong? Can you hear me? Speak to us." She squeezed his fingers against the voice of Father Mitchell ushering parishioners into the sanctuary.

"The paramedics are here." Lynda, Greg's wife, leaned next to Greg, who now knelt across from Rachel. Greg got up, steadied Rachel's shoulders, and helped her to stand. Rachel began to cry.

Michael, unable to speak, tried reaching out with arms that would not move. He had hit the water again, but unlike when he had fallen from the bridge, he floated among jagged memories of a past he didn't understand.

✹ Michael placed a knife and fork beside each dinner plate that evening. Emptiness filled his belly. He had felt it when Greg embraced him earlier that morning. "You're lucky to be alive and have Rachel," Greg had said. He had driven Rachel behind the paramedics, who took Michael to the hospital after he collapsed at the church. He had remained with her until Michael awoke, moments past noon.

Greg told Michael, "Lynda and I are ready to stand by you and Rachel, to watch you renew your vows as soon as you're better." He patted Rachel's shoulder, gripped Michael's, and left. Now, hours after Michael had been released from the hospital, Greg was in the study with Rachel.

Michael folded a napkin and laid it beside Rachel's plate. He set the glasses down, and headed down the hall for the study. As he approached, Greg and Rachel's words grew clearer.

"Do you think he remembers?" Rachel asked.

"Only time will tell. Until then—" Greg said.

"Table's set." Michael entered what had been his office. Bridge plans strewn across the desk a year earlier now stood in the corner by the window. The process of designing bridges no longer held excitement for him. "Sure you don't want to call Lynda—have her join us?" Michael moved to Rachel's side.

"We're heading out to a movie." Greg smiled. He rolled back the sleeve of his trench coat and glanced at his watch. "And you two need time to regroup." He gave Rachel a light kiss, and then walking past Michael, patted his shoulder.

"You can't keep scaring us like this." He turned back to Rachel. "Call if you need anything," he said, and left.

As Michael passed Rachel the garlic bread at dinner, he asked, "What were we like the morning before the accident?"

"Same as any other morning." Rachel sipped her soup and reached for a slice of bread. "Rushed and trying to get to work. Repairing the bridge was on your mind. You wanted to finish the project on—"

"But what was *I* like?" He stared at Rachel.

"I've told you."

The strange emptiness he felt when setting the table arose uncannily.

He's starting to remember, Rachel had said.

Let's wait and see. Time will tell, Greg had responded.

"You're never specific." They'd been through this before. "What was the look on my face?"

Rachel sighed and stood from the table. Michael grabbed her arm. "Let me go!" She pulled back, knocking her bowl of soup onto the floor. "I'll do it." She brushed him aside as she moved to clean the spill.

"No, I've got it." Michael knelt beside her with paper towels. "I said I'll do it." Rachel snatched the towels and began wiping vigorously. She seemed angry, like she had in the memory that had overtaken Michael in the narthex.

"Did we argue the morning before the accident?"

"Who said that?" Rachel turned from wiping.

"I remembered."

"You can either tell me, or—" Michael repeated Greg's words, "time will tell."

Fear colored her brown eyes.

❋ A dull, throbbing pain overtook Michael as he lay in bed next to Rachel later that night. He felt as he had in the narthex before he lost consciousness, but more alert. He gripped the sheets and entered a state between sleep and wakefulness.

He was in a dark room, lying on a hospital bed. A light attached to the wall shone over his head. Rachel stood crying with Greg behind her, his hands on her shoulders, like in the narthex when the paramedics lifted Michael onto the gurney.

He has to make it. Rachel smoothed his hair.

Greg rubbed her shoulders. She tensed. *We argued this morning. It was the same old thing.*

Michael's eyes appeared closed to Rachel in the vision. But he could see her. Her eyes were red and swollen. They held a reflection of him falling from the bridge.

Greg lowered his head. *We have to think positively,* he said.

Rachel turned back. *You don't understand. I don't love Michael anymore. But I need him to live.*

Fighting to free himself from his waking dream, Michael attempted to get out of bed, to move, as he had when lying on the floor of the narthex. Again his arms and legs refused to oblige, and the vision continued.

Rachel kissed Greg's cheek. Michael, in his dream state, felt the passion of his desires flowing through Greg to Rachel. Then, fascinated by the remembered image of Mary's Assumption, Michael felt himself diminished, pulled toward a reality he did not understand.

The vision ended, and Michael fell into a fitful sleep. He awoke the next morning even more confused and angry. He said nothing of the dream to Rachel. He headed off for his appointment with the neurosurgeon.

⁂

The door opened, and Carl Pierson entered, wearing a white coat over his black turtleneck, dark pants, and polished loafers. As always, Pierson's fingers were empty of rings.

"Well, Michael," Pierson laid his chart on the examining table. "I thought you were getting married yesterday—or better yet, renewing your vows. What happened?" Pierson shook Michael's hand.

"I started having memories."

The doctor flicked on his penlight. He touched Michael's cheek. "We were in the kitchen," Michael continued.

"What were you doing?"

"Arguing." Michael stared straight ahead.

"About what?" Pierson shifted the light to Michael's right eye.

I can't...I won't go on like this Michael. Either you make some changes at work or I'll... "I don't remember," Michael lied.

Pierson withdrew the penlight. "Your tests are negative. No blood clots, no apparent abnormalities—"

"Then what could have caused the pain in my head? I felt like I was going to die again."

"You didn't die the first time," Pierson said calmly as he took a seat. "What were you doing right before experiencing the pain?"

Michael turned away. "Talking with a friend—my best man." His voice grew strained as he added, "Rachel was screaming at me in the memory."

"What was she saying?"

"I don't know!" Michael's hands, cold and sweaty, began to shake.

Michael's resentment mounted along with his frustration. He hated that Pierson had declined his invitation to attend the ceremony yesterday. *I'd love to come, Michael, but I have a previous engagement.* Nor had he come into the emergency room to examine Michael after his collapse; he had instructed the emergency room physician to run tests, then called Michael in his hospital room. *Preliminary tests are negative, but I want you in my office tomorrow morning at nine sharp.*

Several times over the year that Pierson had been examining Michael, a nurse had knocked on the door with a message. "Sorry to bother you, Dr. Pierson, but Mrs. Denning's on the line."

"Tell her I'll be right there," Carl had said each time, and then, turning to Michael, excused himself. "This will only take a moment."

On his return, the neurosurgeon would seem preoccupied and disturbed. His brows, normally straight and flat, were furrowed. Pierson looked like a man who had just spoken to his wife about an important issue yet to be resolved.

On one occasion, Pierson had stayed away longer than usual.

When he returned, he brought up the success of Michael's recuperation. "You've come a long way, Michael." He patted Michael's back.

The phone on the wall beside Pierson lit up. An intercom buzz followed. "Yes?" Pierson seemed bothered that their conversation had been interrupted a second time. His smile of moments earlier faded. He excused himself once again.

Fifteen minutes passed before the neurosurgeon's return whereupon he was thorough but markedly quiet—almost withdrawn. Michael sensed sadness combined with anger. He felt a kindred spirit in Carl Pierson, the second of five surgeons to operate on Michael the afternoon of his accident on the Richmond Bridge. Michael's skull had been crushed by a hook intended for the rescue netting used to lift him from the water. During surgery, Pierson had replaced the shattered bone with a metal plate.

Michael had desperately wanted to see Pierson the previous day, when he collapsed before the ceremony.

Michael looked more closely at Pierson's lifesaving hands, empty of rings. The nurse knocked on the door, then entered. "Sorry to bother you, but Mrs. Denning's on line three."

Always Mrs. Denning. On line three. Carl Pierson was having an affair, Michael concluded—like Rachel and Greg.

"Excuse me, Michael. I need to take this." Pierson left and Michael began to feel petulant. Soon he was seething.

"Sorry about that," Pierson said when he came back. He picked up Michael's chart and seated himself once more. "As I was saying, all the tests—"

"I don't care what the tests say!" Michael snapped, then

blurted out what had been on his mind during the doctor's absence. "Are you married?"

Surprised, Pierson asked, "Why do you need to know?"

"Who's 'Mrs. Denning?' Is she a patient or … ?"

She's a good woman. You're lucky to have Rachel, Greg had said. The care in Greg's eyes when he had hugged Michael in the narthex and when he kissed Rachel's forehead on his departure last evening, flashed before Michael. Now, as then, Michael felt alone. That same sense of loneliness had engulfed him during the argument at dinner last night. He felt abandoned by Rachel as she worked to clean up the spill. And he had felt that way out on the bridge the day of the accident too. He had been hanging underneath the bridge, checking pins and screws installed during the recent retrofitting. The delight of freedom he usually felt reflected in sun and sky had been missing.

Michael had been silent for some minutes when he again looked at Pierson. More bewildered than ever, he shook his head, said "I don't know if I want you treating me anymore," and left.

⁂

Michael parked behind the house and entered through the kitchen door. Greg looked up from the kitchen table.

"What are you doing here?" Michael slammed the door.

"Rachel was upset. She called Lynda." Greg's trench coat, wet last evening, was now dry.

"Where's she now?" Michael glanced up to the ceiling. The bedroom he shared with Rachel was directly above.

"They've gone out for a bite to eat."

"And just when are they coming back?"

"Dr. Pierson called." Greg said abruptly, as he stood. "He said that you left his office upset."

"Oh?"

"Have you considered seeing someone? Michael, what's going on? Have they found something you're not telling us about? Rachel said the emergency room tests were clear."

"I'm fine." Michael stared into the eyes of his best man. His friend. "Maybe there's something you and Rachel ought to tell me, and perhaps Lynda." Like Dr. Pierson, Greg was startled and confused. "I know what happened between you and Rachel," Michael said. "You two are having an affair."

"I don't know who told you this—" Greg flashed his palms.

Michael grabbed Greg's collar, and drew back his fist.

The kitchen door opened. "What's going on?" Rachel rushed to Michael and Greg.

"Perhaps we should leave." Greg joined Lynda, then turned to Rachel with a questioning look.

"I'll be okay."

"So this is what we've come to," Michael said. "You having to tell Greg that it's okay for you to stay here with me, your husband." He pointed to his chest. "You remember me? We were going to renew our wedding vows? Then again, you don't love me anymore. You just need me to stay alive!" Rachel gasped. Greg and Lynda exchanged looks. "You and Greg are having an affair!" Michael pointed at Rachel. Lynda whispered to Greg. Rachel began to cry.

"When I was in the hospital," Michael said, "Greg was standing behind you with his hands on your shoulders. And you said—"

Rachel's eyes widened, as if in recognition of what Michael had yet to understand. "You two go home." She ushered Greg and Lynda to the door. "I'll call you later."

"Are you sure you're going to be alright?" Greg said, before walking through the door. He touched her shoulders as he had the previous day, and then last evening.

"Get your hands off my wife!" Michael rushed toward them.

"That's enough!" Rachel extended her arms like a bridge, again separating the two. Greg and Lynda left, and Rachel closed the door.

Michael's vision blurred. The interplay of images in Michael's head, that of Christ's Ascension and the Holy Mother's Assumption, reached its most intense. He shook his head and fought for clarity. "I want to know the truth," he demanded.

Rachel scanned his face and took a deep breath. "Greg was with me that night at the hospital after they brought you in." She folded her hands. "They told me they didn't know how extensive your injuries were. You had only a thirty-percent chance of living. I didn't know what to do."

Michael wanted to scream, "Pray!" But he knew Rachel had done that. He was scared. Rachel stared down at the table from which she had knocked the bowl of soup onto the floor last night. Michael felt light-headed. What few memories he had pieced together splintered. He swallowed the tears clogging his throat.

"I called Greg when I got the call about the accident," Rachel said. "He met me at the hospital—stayed all night. They said you might not make it through the night. And, I'd just—" Rachel stopped herself. Before Michael could urge her to go on, she gathered her resolve.

"You said we needed to get a divorce."

Michael grew more anxious. He didn't know the person about whom she was speaking.

"I'd just spoken to my lawyer." Rachel began to cry. "I never thought it would come to this. You never gave out threats, always did what you said. It's what I loved about you."

"Don't you love me now? I'm not that man."

"But who *are* you? How do I know *he* won't come back?"

Thirteen months had come and gone since the accident. Michael wanted to get on with his life. At thirty-seven, he had a large part of his life left to live. Not once had he inspected any of the bridge plans folded and stored in the corner. Memories of his body feeling on fire when he'd hit the Pacific came to the forefront each time he approached his desk or thought of unfolding his drawings.

"I've told you I don't know that person—I can't remember him!" He clutched at Rachel's shoulders.

She stepped back. "It was hard accepting what you'd said that morning. It was even harder not knowing whether you'd live."

"I'll find a therapist, Rachel. We can work this out."

The truth-teller in Rachel retreated, leaving Michael ignorant of what or whom he was fighting.

Michael stood in line at the coffee shop, sullen and frustrated. Caught up in memories of his angry exchange with Greg, and then Rachel, Michael didn't look at the man in front of him, just wished he would get his coffee and go. Latte paid for, the gentleman turned around, and Michael found himself facing Carl Pierson. Michael lowered his head.

"Are you feeling better?" Pierson placed his hand upon Michael's shoulder and led him to a table in the corner.

"I accused Rachel of having an affair with Greg," he said unhappily. He explained what Rachel had said about the morning before the accident, "I told her we needed to divorce." Michael shook his head. "How could I have been that way to Rachel? And Greg and I go way back. Our fathers were good men. They loved our mothers."

Again Michael regarded Carl's fingers, empty of ornament. And then it hit him. Rachel's fingers had been empty of a wedding band in Michael's vision. With sickening lucidity, he felt Rachel's indomitable patience fading. "She's going to leave; I can feel it. I need her." He clenched his fists, something he hadn't done in thirteen months.

Michael believed Rachel but couldn't remember asking for the divorce. His outburst with Pierson and then with Greg had bad been his first experiences of anger since the accident.

"I've never stopped loving Rachel." Michael was frightened.

Again Michael stared at the bare fingers of Pierson's left hand around his latte. No rings.

"Dr. Pierson, do you think I'm a good man, a good person?"

"Of course."

Michael felt horrible for what he had said to Pierson—the way he had left the neurosurgeon's office.

"You've been through a lot this last year and a half," Pierson said. "Most people don't even survive a hit to the Pacific, never mind that crack in your skull." Michael ran his hand across his bald head. His hair had been an inch thick before the accident.

Pierson sat his cup on the table between them. "The real question is, what do you think?"

Had Rachel told Pierson about their troubles? Did he know about Rachel and Greg? Had Greg spoken with him after Michael had burst from the office?

"The events in our lives have many facets. Some we see. Others we miss, can't comprehend without the help of others." Pierson told Michael about an incident over in the City. "It was at a restaurant where a lot of bigwigs take clients. Blackened windows, private. You know the deal." Michael nodded yes, but struggled to see how the story related to his lack of memory.

"There was an outburst. One of the patrons, a woman, tried to slit the throat of the man at her table. I don't know if they were married or not. Another woman tried to calm her. She was about to hand over the knife, then she went for the man's neck again. A second man rushed over and stopped her.

"After that, police and paramedics took her away. The first thing that popped into my mind when I heard about this was that if you asked people what they saw, everyone would give a different story. Even those sitting at the same table. We each have our own take on what's happening," Pierson said. "*My* perspective and *yours*." He touched his chest and then Michael's. "And then there is what all of this means. That's what you're struggling to figure out. Between you and Rachel."

The dread on Rachel's face when she recounted what Michael had said settled in his stomach like a hard mass. "I don't want to lose her. If I push too hard, she's going to say it's the *old* me."

"The old you never left. The accident just unearthed a part of you that you never acknowledged."

Pierson's words both excited and terrified Michael. Over the last year, he had been the one who cooked, while Rachel returned to her job as a CPA at an Oakland firm. He had also begun gardening and reading. Michael liked being at home. It felt safe. He had searched out several consulting jobs that he could do from home, allowing him flexibility for any children they might have. He wanted children. It was time for Rachel and him to start a family.

"Rachel's holding something back," he said. "She's told me a lot, but there's something missing. I can feel it, just like when walking across a bridge. It has a feel."

Michael absorbed his own words. The stained-glass reflections of Christ and the Holy Mother rose in Michael. The reality of his two selves merged.

What we feel in someone's presence helps us to understand them and ourselves. Those had been Carl Pierson's words. Rachel was Michael's bridge to their past—his past—the Michael before the fall. He needed to hear about her pain since the accident.

❧ Michael carefully lowered himself onto the bed where Rachel lay asleep. He stroked her face. She turned over and opened her eyes. After a moment, she softly said, "I didn't want you to go that morning. I was scared—like all the other days—afraid that you'd get hurt.

"You wanted a child; I resisted." She placed her hand over his. "You always wanted to be up there with the men. *Certainty.*" She said the word often used by Michael.

Children solidified a family, bound a husband and wife for eternity.

Michael's fingers curved into a fist once more. He tightened his jaw as he had the morning before falling from the bridge. A memory rose of Rachel making ultimatums.

I'm not going to keep up this charade, Michael. I don't want to be a widow at thirty-five. Certainly not one with a child.

Who says you have to? Don't you realize what it took for me to get to this place in my career? Like I said, if the heat's too much, get out! You knew what I did when we married.

Why do you have to let it kill you? At some point everyone has to—

I'm thirty-six fucking years old, Rachel! My career's ahead of me.

That is, if you live. Martin fell last year. And then Caruthers two weeks ago—

I have to go to work.

Michael had stormed past her. Then, as now, her words followed him, rang in his head. *I had the abortion.*

Now sitting up in bed, Rachel embraced him. He did not feel her holding him.

He began to shake. Vulnerability consumed the man he was now, as it had then. Rachel's voice from that morning rang in his ears.

Greg's drawing up the divorce papers, Michael. I won't live like this. I can't.

⁂

Minutes passed now as then, the time it took to breathe in and out. Michael felt himself falling toward the Pacific again. Enough time to cut his harness—a lifetime.

Certainty. The word roamed his mind. Michael felt Rachel's pain—and his.

Michael knew that his mother had planned to abort him after leaving his father. And then the procedure, in those days illegal, had failed.

Michael had contemplated the knife all morning before

the accident. He had felt so weak upon reaching the Richmond Bridge for work. The prospect of moving through life without Rachel terrified him. That afternoon following lunch his harness loosened.

Slipping. Falling.

Rachel now pulled him tighter, but Michael didn't feel her holding on. He was drifting, remembering the need to ascend, to be consumed, assumed.

Orange light over the Pacific encompassed him as it had moments before he hit the water. The bitterness of death filled his nose. Michael wasn't ascending. He took in a gasp of air, remembered cutting the harness, his hands, his need to die.

And then there had been the spirit of the unborn child, his and Rachel's, filled with the angst of Michael's father, alone and abandoned, searching, roaming, reaching for convergence with Michael who *had* been born, a boy without a father, a husband deserted by his wife, a man with no child to carry on his name.

"I'm sorry," Rachel said. Michael didn't hear her as he fought for breath. Last impressions of Christ's Ascension and Mary's Assumption faded, leaving the vision of a small infant held by his mother, the two moving toward a blue light, one dissipating into clear white. He wished he could cut the harness again.

Three Movements

Ariane wanted to touch the image in the mirror, but she worried that Gayle would go away. Gayle spoke. "Tony needed to be with me."

"But I needed to see you. There was so much to say."

"So, tell me now."

The tingling in Ariane's fingers grew stronger. "I miss you, our talks. No one understood me like you did," she said.

Gayle smiled as she never had in session. Her chestnut face glowed with a strange light, soft and hazy. But Ariane could see her clearly. Gayle was in the mirror, her body healed, the cancer gone.

"Have you spoken to Jack?" Gayle prompted.

"About what?"

"About what you wanted to tell me."

How could she know? Ariane's body stiffened. Gayle seemed to move closer, as if to emerge from the mirror. Without conscious thought, Ariane stepped closer. Her chin raised as if tipped up by Gayle's hand. Ariane felt the brush of her fingertip. And yet Gayle's image remained enclosed in the mirror.

"You're a good person, Dr. Ariane Gadsen—a good person and an excellent therapist. But excellence is often the enemy of good." Gayle's smile began to fade. The glow around her dimmed.

Ariane lowered her eyelids, absorbing Gayle's words. She opened them and Gayle was no more. She saw only the reflection of her face, her sadness tangible upon it.

Ariane cursed a second time as she fumbled while hooking the strand of pearls about her neck. She was standing before her bedroom mirror.

Jack, in his black tuxedo, came up behind her and gently took the ends of the necklace from her fingers. "Did you get Jill's message?" He secured the clasp. "She called Wednesday about the Jack and Jill gathering."

"Gathering? Jill?" Ariane met his eyes in the mirror, empty now of Gayle's image.

"She left a message asking if Kent would play. It's on Sunday, a week from tomorrow." It was then Saturday evening and Ariane and Jack were headed out to meet Jill and her husband Alan for dinner. "I think he would enjoy your accompanying him."

"It's such short notice." Ariane crossed to the bed and snatched up the clothing she had laid out. She wasn't ready for an evening with Jill and Alan, nor did she want to contemplate playing the piano before a crowd. She didn't want to play at all, but playing the piano was the only thing that took her mind off Gayle.

Jack followed her as she moved toward the hooks on the closet door. He settled his palms upon her shoulders. "I love your playing. It's soothing." Ariane wriggled her shoulder from under Jack's hand as she hung up her bathrobe.

"Did you see your therapist this week?" he asked.

"Can we not talk about this right now?" Ariane had stopped going to her therapist. She left the closet, Jack close behind.

"It's been nearly eight months," Jack said. Unable to hide the devastation Gayle's death had wrought upon her, Ariane knew Jack had discovered how attached she was to Gayle.

"She wasn't your only client," Jack said.

"I'm just tired."

"No you're not." Jack grasped Ariane's arm and turned her around. "You're grieving. Like something inside of you died with Gayle Clayton. For Christ's sake, she was your patient, Ariane, not your family."

Ariane yearned to tell him about seeing Gayle's image in the mirror. She had stopped going to therapy when Gayle ceased appearing in the mirror.

"Would you like to resume the divorce proceedings?" Jack's words ambushed Ariane, as she knew hers had when she had asked Jack for a divorce.

"No. But I could ask the same of you."

"I didn't bring it up the first time."

Jack had been a good and responsible friend beyond loving her, but Ariane felt his patience thinning.

"You said the divorce would let you figure things out," Jack reminded her. "Help you understand why you had made it this far despite the loss of your parents." During their first date Ariane had shared with Jack the pain of losing her father, who was killed in Vietnam. She then explained how her mother had lost her battle with cancer a year later, when Ariane had been ten. These days it seemed Jack's love reminded Ariane too much of what her mother had lost when Ariane's father died.

Jack again placed his hand upon Ariane's shoulder. "I love you. Isn't that enough?"

"Tell him." Gayle's voice encouraged. Ariane glanced at the mirror, which held no signs of Gayle's face. She had never heard Gayle's voice when not before the mirror. And over a month had passed since Ariane last saw Gayle's reflection.

"As much as I'm glad to see you take some time off, I'm worried." Jack seemed oblivious to Ariane's agitation.

Ariane returned to the mirror and stared into the reflection of her own eyes. Gayle's face took shape, obliterating Ariane's. That too was a new development. In the past Gayle had always stood behind Ariane. The dead woman now faced Ariane as if Ariane had willed Gayle to appear and she, herself, to leave.

"What are you doing here?" Ariane whispered to Gayle through clenched teeth.

"Trying to keep you from making the biggest mistake of your life," came the response.

Again Jack approached Ariane and stood behind her in Gayle's usual position. "Talk to me. Tell me what's going on in that little head of yours." Appearing unaware of Gayle's presence, he nuzzled Ariane's neck.

I'm going crazy. Ariane threw back her head, closed her eyes, and tore her fingers through her hair. Jack massaged her shoulders. Ariane willed herself to relax. She took in the warmth of his palms, let it spread over her until she felt safe.

"Now that's more like it." Gayle's words pierced Ariane's calm. Ariane popped her head up and stared into the mirror. She saw only herself, bewilderment stirring in her eyes, and Jack behind her with his soft, ever-present smile.

Holding Ariane's shoulders he turned her to face him. "I'll be alright," she said, pulling away. "Just give me more time."

"And when that's up, what next?" Jack seized Ariane's arms, shook her like a parent whose child had run across the street without looking and was nearly struck by a car. "There's so much I don't know about you. Tell me. I want to listen." Ariane's heart raced. "Let me love you." Jack pulled her to his chest. Ariane opened her eyes and saw only Jack. Her knees weakened.

"It was so much easier to give love than receive it," Gayle said.

Jack nudged her chin with his knuckle, brought his lips to hers. The hardness in Ariane's chest grew soft.

"Now that's more like it," Gayle said again.

※

Sunday, a week later, Ariane slid her fingers down the keyboard and completed the piano accompaniment to her son Kent's violin sonata. She stood and bowed to the applause of nearly a hundred brown faces. Turning to Kent, she bowed again. The clapping grew louder. To the audience's pleasure, Kent extended his hand and invited Ariane to a second bow. A shiver spilled down her spine.

The crowd continued clapping and smiling. Though anxious, as she had been when Jack discovered she played the piano—and quite well—Ariane now felt warm inside.

"This is how your life is supposed to be," Gayle's voice reminded her. Ariane maintained her smile. "Take it in." Gayle's presence, though a surprise, comforted Ariane. During the past week she had come to Ariane away from the mirror, speaking to her each day. "Let it heal you." Her voice was now coming from the crowd. Ariane smiled at Kent and then Jack. She felt proud of loving, and of being loved.

Most of the guests had moved out onto the patio as Ariane gathered Kent's music and got ready to put it in a folder with her own. She reached for his violin case on the coffee table. A voice said, "You played wonderfully. Are you a professional?"

Startled, she whipped around. A tall man stood in the doorway. "Do I know you?"

"How long have you played?" The man's tender smile and willowy eyelashes gave him an otherworldly air. "Your accompaniment was subtle and sustaining, not overpowering." He walked toward her.

"Are you a musician?" she asked. He still had not answered her earlier question.

"Just a lover of music—all art, for that matter."

"Thank you for the compliment. Perhaps I'll see you again." She took hold of the handle to Kent's violin case.

"You haven't answered my question."

"Nor you mine." The man was making her uncomfortable. Ariane turned back.

He stopped her by extending his hand. "Renaldo Baptiste."

Regretting her haughtiness, Ariane shook his hand. "Ariane Gadsen. But then I guess you already knew that." Jill, the host, had introduced mother and son as they prepared to play. "Does your wife belong to Jack and Jill?" The gathering consisted of members of Jack and Jill, an organization for mothers.

"She did." Renaldo lowered his head.

"So you're friends with Jill?" Divorced women's ex-husbands were always trying to maintain social bonds and connection with their wives by attending various events after the decree.

Renaldo touched his forehead as if to dispel some confusion. "You have to forgive me; it's been a crazy year. I don't always keep names —"

"That's fine." Ariane sensed the matter of Renaldo's wife was better left alone. "Perhaps I'll see you again." She did not want to encounter him again. Yet never one for brutal honesty, Ariane picked up Kent's violin, shook Renaldo Baptiste's hand, and left.

Raven Clarke, another member of Jack and Jill, joined Ariane on the far side of the deck. "Well, another one of your secrets is out." Raven set down her plate of salmon and hugged Ariane. "I've been meaning to call you. Jack told me you were taking some time off," Raven said. "Jill tells me you're back with us in Jack and Jill."

"I am." Ariane didn't know for how long. She enjoyed Jack and Jill, what the women who belonged to it were about — accomplished and educated mothers who exercised the options of equality while remaining committed to family. There was no one she could talk to, no one she felt would understand. The organization also bored her, created a sense of confusion.

Ariane gave a sardonic smile. That her husband, Jack, and the host of the event, Jill, held the very names of the mother's group, "Jack and Jill," was synchronistic at the very least. That she had met this Renaldo at an event sponsored under the auspices of the association was, at a stretch, serendipitous. But Ariane didn't believe in positive discoveries, nor did she give into caprice. Her life revolved around death and dying, the certain and the unavoidable—she helped people die, and assisted those left behind in making sense of life's greatest paradox, death. Most people, unless personally affected, didn't want to talk about the subject.

Mere days before entering the hospital, never to leave, Gayle said, "It's like you are a pariah, when you are dying and everybody knows it. I saw it in their eyes at work—pity and fear. That's when I knew it was time to go."

"And how is it being home?" Ariane had asked.

"Tony's great." Gayle smiled. "He's wonderful."

Raven smiled at Ariane's greeting. "It's so good to see you." Another psychotherapist, Raven hadn't worked since the birth of her middle child, age thirteen, and several months earlier had given birth to her youngest daughter.

Ariane said, "I don't know how you do it. You look well—three kids, a husband—and Jack and Jill." Ariane waved her hand as if to encompass the room and its occupants.

"Believe me, I've got my own private mental hospital at home," Raven said. "Kaarin just went through this spell of crying—every night. Nothing would calm her except sleeping next to me." Raven's eyes with flecks of green dulled. "Then again, if it means they won't have to seek therapy for my lack of attention..." Ariane nodded in agreement and patted Raven's hand. Much of their work was caring for their families. Unlike Raven, Ariane had always placed Jack and Kent second to her clients until Gayle's death.

She raised her wine glass, said, "I met Renaldo Baptiste," and took a sip.

"Oh." Raven checked to see if anyone was listening, then in a low voice murmured, "It's really sad."

"The divorce?"

Raven searched Ariane's face for a moment, green eyes sparkling. "That's right...you wouldn't know." Ariane had taken a leave of absence from Jack and Jill during the last year. Agreeing to accompany Kent signaled her return. "Renaldo's wife died. She was in Jack and Jill."

"You're kidding."

"It happened sometime last year. I'm not up on all the details. He's a really nice man. So is his son. Drew encouraged Renaldo to petition for membership to help his son."

"He's an attorney?" Raven's husband, Drew, was a lawyer.

"No, Renaldo's a writer. His wife was the attorney." They'd been divorced," Raven said. "He was with her when she died."

Ariane sipped her zinfandel and mulled that over. Ariane considered her last months with Gayle. Gayle's husband, Tony Clayton, had loved her and had kept Gayle to himself in her last hours. Ariane was angry with him for denying her even a moment with Gayle.

Raven said, still talking about Renaldo and his wife, "They apparently got back together when she became ill from the chemo."

"It'll do that." Ariane recalled her clients' struggles with what many viewed as another battle in their war to stay alive. "When they get sick from the chemo is when many of my clients realize they're dying."

It hadn't been that way with Gayle. She had entered Ariane's office on the first visit stating, "I'm dying, and there's a lot I need to say."

Ariane said quietly, "My last client died from cancer—breast cancer."

The jade-colored light in Raven's eyes again faded. Her irises ran soft, almost clear. She said, "Jack told me you went through a rough time."

For a moment Ariane thought she saw the image of

Gayle's face in Raven's eyes. "It's why I took some time off."
Raven touched her arm. Ariane wanted to pull away. She
didn't have three children to keep her busy, nor did she care
to immerse herself in Jack's world to the depths at which
Raven tread Drew's. Everyone knew that Raven's husband,
a busy lawyer, demanded that she remain ever by his side,
even when he met with clients outside the office.

Rumors circulated that sixteen years earlier Drew had
rescued Raven from a foreign client, and made her his wife.
The client, a mysterious man from the East, had been Raven's
lover. In exchange for Drew's successful court defense that
gained the man his freedom, or so it was said, the client
agreed to leave Raven and never return.

Ariane recently heard by way of Jack that a fight had
broken out in a restaurant where Drew was engaged with
a client in one of those after-hours meetings. The vicious
exchange occurred between two other patrons. A woman
had tried to stab the man at her table. Without hesitation,
Raven had gone and spoken to the woman. Drew, right
behind Raven, had restrained the woman and grabbed the
knife when Raven failed at enticing it from the woman, thus
saving the man's throat from being slashed.

Ariane wished she could sink into Jack's love the way it
seemed Raven had settled into Drew's protection. At times
she wished she had no clients to attend, had only Jack and
their son to set her mind to. Yet even now with this imposed
leave of absence, she wrestled with unsettling thoughts,
questioning the meaning and purpose of her life. Why had
she lived, reached the age of forty-two, when her parents
were thirty-nine and forty when they died?

Ariane had felt empty when she reached her forty-first
birthday. Enter Gayle Clayton providing Ariane respite
from solitary confinement to the memory of her mother's
death, with the loss of her father as prison warden.

Ariane had survived the death of her father by playing
the piano with her mother. The two would sit side-by-side.

The music created by her mother's nimble fingers bound them as her mother sang along.

Her mother's death a year later left Ariane's fingers lost, searching for more experienced hands to accompany her on the piano and in life. Ariane stopped playing the piano upon entering college.

Jack, adamant that Kent find a way to express his feelings beyond sports, enrolled Kent in weekly group violin lessons. Hearing the music of Kent's practicing irritated Ariane to near exasperation. Then one afternoon, Kent, two years into his lessons, played a simple sonata. Ariane's mother had taught her that piece. She left the kitchen where she had been preparing dinner, went to the piano, and accompanied him. For the first time in a long while, it felt good and safe to play—as if her mother sat beside her.

When they finished, she met Jack's brown eyes, which registered shock. "That was beautiful. You never told me. Why?"

The five weeks Ariane hadn't seen or heard Gayle in the mirror had been the loneliest since childhood. Ariane had felt her mother's presence when listening to Gayle. It had been that way before Gayle died, too. The intensity of her mother's presence increased each time Gayle appeared in the bedroom mirror. Bereft during the month of Gayle's absence, Ariane sought refuge in playing the piano, accompanying Kent as he played the violin.

⁂ Ariane acknowledged Raven's soft smile, wished for strength to tell Raven her story. And then the familiarity of a voice pulled Ariane from her reverie. "Raven." Ariane turned around. "Ah, so we meet again," Renaldo Baptiste said.

Raven reached for Renaldo's hand. He in turn kissed her cheek. "Renaldo, this is Ariane, one of our members."

"And the lady who accompanied her son." Renaldo flashed that sad smile, leaving Ariane uneasy. Knowing of his loss left her with a troubled kinship beyond the fact that they had lost loved ones to terminal illnesses. "We met earlier," he said.

"Ariane told me." Raven smiled at Ariane as if to coax her into conversation with Renaldo.

"I told her she plays well," Renaldo said. "As does her son." He put his hands together and gave a half bow. Ariane felt him offering an olive branch for the discomfort she felt in his presence, despite his gentlemanliness.

Raven turned her head slightly toward Drew, who a moment earlier was talking among the cluster of men by the door, and now approached the three. He shook hands with Renaldo, then said to Raven, "I think we need to go."

Raven hugged Ariane again. "It's been so nice seeing you. Don't remain scarce. Now that you've taken some time off, we'll have to meet for breakfast at the Egg Shoppe. I'll catch you up on all the goings-on."

"That would be nice." Ariane smiled, but knew she held no intentions of taking up Raven's offer.

"And you." Raven hugged Renaldo, kissed his cheek. "Call if you need anything."

"Yes, please do." Drew added as he shook Renaldo's hand.

"Thanks," he said. And the two left.

"They're a really nice couple." Renaldo resettled his attention on Ariane.

"Yes, they are." Aware that Renaldo had come to know Raven and Drew's kindness through his wife's death, Raven would not venture into his relationship with them.

He said, "So you and Raven are friends?"

"Our kids go to the same school. And as you see, we're both members of Jack and Jill."

"So was my wife."

"Raven told me." Ariane felt herself growing tense under Renaldo's scrutiny.

"It seems like you've been away from the organization for a while."

Ariane's fingers began to tingle. "The last year's been busy." She surveyed the room for Jack.

"Do you teach music?" Renaldo seemed truly interested. "I've been wanting my son to take lessons. Ever since my wife died—"

"I'm sorry to hear about your wife. But—" The words spilled from Ariane; she could not stop them. "It seems my husband and son are looking for me." Jack and Kent had entered the room.

She extended her hand to Renaldo. "It was nice talking with you," she said, then crossed the room to tell Jack she was ready to leave.

Within minutes, they reached their home on Skyline, less than a mile from Jill and her husband Alan's house. When Ariane entered, she found the flames of votive candles making a path.

"Follow the yellow brick road," Jack said, when Ariane turned to him. She edged down the hall, which was all aglow, and felt the eyes and spirits of all whom she had shepherded into death.

A hundred or more candles lit the kitchen. Jack placed a bowl of soup before her. She selected a slice of Madras bread from the basket, and then surveyed the platter of duck garnished with asparagus.

Jack slid the plate of salad between them. "This is enough for two. I thought we'd share it." He sat. "You'll have to call J.L. tomorrow and thank him," he said. J.L. was a private chef. He had prepared and laid out the meal while Ariane and Jack were at Jill's gathering. In years past, he had cooked Friday meals for Ariane and Jack. Friday dinners had been a ritual at the outset of their marriage—a moment of retrieval, of themselves and each other, from Ariane's budding psychotherapy practice and Jack's partnership with the architecture and engineering firm he had established with Alan.

Jack's brown face was somber, guarded in the glow of the room.

"You never told me what you wanted for your birthday." Jack brought a blue box from the darkness. Inside lay a bracelet of twenty small diamonds set off by two oval sapphires. He placed it around Ariane's wrist and engaged the clasp. Ariane felt herself slipping into the state of agitation she'd felt when with Renaldo Baptiste. She admired the bracelet, its diamonds and sapphires glittering in the candlelight.

The sparkles reminded Ariane of the light from the candle she had used to invoke her mother's presence.

While Ariane was living with her mother's brother and his wife, she would sit in the glow of a candle lighting her room and stare at her mother's picture.

She hadn't known about her mother's second mastectomy. Her mother's sister-in-law had thought it too much to explain to a ten-year-old, less than twelve months after her father's death in Vietnam.

She was disappointed each time she blew out the candle having heard and felt nothing. Ariane remembered that disappointment each time she held a child in the wake of their parent's death. She worried about Tony Clayton not having allowed their daughter to be with Gayle in her final moments. And now there was Renaldo Baptiste. Ariane had just met him. His suffering was palpable. Ariane felt the throb of his loss through the wound rent in her by Gayle's death.

⁂

Ariane touched the bracelet. Her eyes filled with tears.

"Thank you for accompanying Kent this afternoon," Jack said. His demeanor resembled what she imagined Drew would display with Raven in private. Ariane wanted so much to become Jack's Raven.

"He's our son."

"Still, it was nice." He murmured. She inclined her head to Jack's lingering but wary smile. "I was just supporting Kent."

"There's an art to supporting people—not overpowering them—just being there."

Tremors rose from beneath Ariane's polished exterior. That's what Renaldo had said. Ariane had been acutely aware, when standing before him, of the isolation and abandonment she felt in the wake of Gayle's death. Renaldo seemed alienated too. His wife had died. That, along with his persistent compliments about her playing, had painfully annoyed her—that and the all-too-familiar sadness. Ariane had carried that sadness since her mother died.

Jack leaned forward and kissed Ariane's cheek.

"Jack loves you. Take it in." Gayle's voice sounded in her head. For the first time in a long while, Ariane received comfort and affection, instead of giving it.

Jack whispered, "Aunt Winifred said you were as tough as nails when it came to death. Perhaps you could give some of that strength to life and the living."

Jack had met Ariane at his uncle's grave site. He had been eager to meet the woman whom his aunt credited with easing his uncle's acceptance of death.

The candles lighting the kitchen flickered in unison, as if a breath from the beyond had blown upon them, yet instead of snuffing them out, invigorated their flames. Jack lifted her wrist. "Each one of the diamonds represents two years of your life. The sapphires are for our last two together."

The ten-year-old inside Ariane peered through veils of pain at Jack. Tears filled her eyes. "I never wanted a divorce."

"Why did you ask for it?"

"I don't know," the little girl said again. Ariane couldn't understand that any more than she understood why life had prevented her from bidding farewell to her mother.

⁂

Ariane conducted Gayle's first session two days after Ariane had turned forty-one. Her birthday had been a private nightmare. Her parents had not lived beyond forty. Why had she lived and they not? What was the meaning of her life, filled with so much death?

Cancer had severed Ariane's connection with her mother and herself. Only when watching death creep over those it was about to devour did Ariane feel alive. She stood by people facing death when others, often their family members, caught in their own web of fears, abandoned them.

Ariane was tired. She wanted to become a part of the living, to open up and take in life—not to live in fear that Jack or Kent might die in the next moment. She perpetually contemplated the darkness that she knew with certainty lurked behind every corner her husband and son approached. It was a foregone conclusion in Ariane's mind that it would snatch them, and return her adult self to the ten-year-old girl, lost and searching, that she had been on the day her mom died.

Ariane had worked with Gayle during the twelve months between her forty-first and forty-second birthdays.

Jack searched Ariane's eyes for an entry point. They were lying in bed, the room dark. For the first time since her mother's death, Ariane heard a piano duet they'd often played. Jack drew close, placed his naked chest against hers. Something snapped within Ariane. "Not now." She rolled away.

Where is Gayle's voice? Her presence would give Ariane the strength to open up and let go.

Ariane held her face with her hands and peered at Jack, who seemed lost and frustrated. "I just need—"

"What?" Jack sat up. "I want my wife back!"

The omnipresence of Jack's love was imposing. It had taken everything within Ariane to accept the bracelet and Jack's accompanying affection. Her memories were excruciating, the music too real—like Renaldo and his pain—too alive. Unlike Gayle's voice, the memories were taking Ariane back to her mother, where she couldn't stay.

"I'm afraid," Ariane blurted.

"That's it. Keep talking," Gail coaxed.

"Afraid of losing you—like my mother."

"But I'm here with you now." Jack touched her throat tenderly. "You've got to let this thing with Gayle Clayton go. I can't keep going back and forth like this. One minute you're letting me love you, I'm feeling your love. The next you're asking for a divorce. I never know what to expect. I want this woman, her ghost, out of our lives."

Ariane slipped from Jack's grasp. She heard music in her head—the sonata she had played earlier with Kent—and then as she had played it with her mother three decades ago. Jack knitted his brows. Ariane had not told him how she learned to play the piano, about the music she made with her mother, nor the circumstances surrounding her mother's passing. Ariane had not seen her mother for the last three weeks of her life

The phone rang. Jack's voice was terse as he spoke into the receiver. He massaged his temples. "She's here—" He stood in front of the window across the room. The moonlight contrasted with the silhouette of his body. "But this is not a good time."

Ariane could feel the words on the other end speeding up, as the caller tried to make their case to Jack. She padded over to him; he slapped the cordless into her palm.

"Ariane. It's Ellis. Sorry to bother you, but Gayle Clayton's husband left a message. It seems that Gayle's husband has decided to execute her last will and testament. He wants to speak with her therapist." Eager and yet fearful, Ariane sank into a state of guarded hopefulness. "I haven't called him back," Ellis continued. "Whatever you need me to say—"

"No. I'll see him." Ariane had never seen Gayle's husband, whom Gayle referred to as Tony, during Gayle's year of sessions. Ariane had never even spoken to him on the phone.

⁂

The light on the office wall flashed red. Mr. Clayton had arrived. Ariane pushed back from her desk and walked to the door to greet him. "Mr. Clayton." The man turned from the water dispenser, and Ariane recognized him. "Renaldo Baptiste?" She searched for her place in the reality of the moment.

He stepped toward her cautiously. "You look different this morning." He extended his hand.

"But Ellis said you were—"

"Gayle Clayton's husband. I am. Clayton was Gayle's maiden name. She used it all the time. It was one of our points of contention. She also liked calling me Tony—my middle name is Anthony. Ever since she died, though, I have avoided being called that." Renaldo's gaze retreated into shadows of an almost unending sadness.

Minutes later, Ariane slid to the edge of her seat. "This must be very awkward for you. Us having met yesterday in a social setting, and then—"

"What about you?"

"You're my concern."

Renaldo surveyed the white walls of the rectangular office. His black eyes with drooping lashes appeared lifeless as they found their way back to Ariane. "You cared a lot for my wife—she appreciated your patience."

"You mean that I didn't probe her about you?" Ariane's anger at Renaldo for not having allowed her to visit Gayle surfaced. Finding out that she had met him yesterday made it all the more awkward. "It was my job." She popped a mint in her mouth.

"You made a stink about not being able to see her."

⚜

Ariane had rushed to Alta Bates on receiving Gayle's message. The nurse said on Ariane's arrival, "The family requests no visitors," mentioning neither Tony nor Renaldo. "I'll deliver the message to her husband."

"But I'm her therapist."

"Only the immediate family is permitted." The nurse's face softened. She declined to reveal Gayle's room number, adding, "It's a difficult time for them right now."

"I need to see Gayle. Who's supporting her daughter?"

The nurse appeared confused, a question hanging behind her words, "The family is taking care of that."

Ariane walked away, the nurse's words draining into the rawness of her wounds ripped open by Gayle's terminal illness. Her face and arms felt as if they were pin cushions being stung by pins.

She knew that despite the nurse's demeanor, she suffered too when a patient died. Here this moment, breathing and talking—or simply with eyes open and staring—then gone the next. No one was immune.

⁂

Renaldo hunched his elbows upon his knees, and interwove his fingers. Tears fell from his face onto the olive-colored carpet, each drop creating a dark spot around where the others had descended.

"It was unfair of me to exclude people from seeing Gayle when she was dying." He raised his head.

"I wasn't angry at you—or anyone for that matter. It was just that—" Renaldo said. "My son and I were losing the one person—"

"Your son?" Gayle made the connection with what Raven had said the night before. But Gayle had said she had a daughter. Ariane recalled the confusion on the nurse's face, and felt the primitive sadness she had experienced when learning Gayle had died. It arose yesterday afternoon when she was with Renaldo and then when she saw him turn from the watercooler, and knew that he was Gayle's husband, also known as Tony Clayton. She wanted to ask him to leave, but as with Ariane, death had stripped him of seeing life.

Renaldo went on as if she had not spoken. "It was never my idea—the separation or the divorce."

"Divorce." Ariane drug her hands through her hair. Gayle had said nothing of leaving nor divorcing her husband, and always spoke of him lovingly.

Renaldo said, "Gayle's mother left when she was ten. Her father died a year later. When I met Gayle, she was the most independent person I had ever seen—wouldn't let me open a door for her, nor let her pass into a building before me."

Ariane leaned back in her chair. It was all so confusing. A patient had lied to her. That had never happened before. And Ariane had been attached to her.

"I realize now she was protecting the little girl inside." Renaldo surveyed the office then fixed his eyes upon the wall behind Ariane. "The story Gayle gave you is what she told everyone—even me." Ariane forced herself to breathe.

The depth of Gayle's dishonesty settled upon her. The woman Raven had spoken of yesterday was Gayle Clayton, Ariane's client. And Renaldo Baptiste, whose sadness had so affected Ariane, was Gayle's husband. Ariane let out a heavy sigh.

"Facing death makes people strange." Renaldo leaned back upon the couch, rested his hands upon his thighs. "I was at work when Gayle called. She had been gone about a year. She was sobbing. I figured it was a prank. Was about to hang up, then Gayle spoke. 'Please come.'"

"I rushed over to her apartment, found her crumpled in the corner of her bedroom. She could barely speak. At first I thought she had lost a case and was devastated. Then she said, 'I've got breast cancer. I'm dying.'" Renaldo's voice shook. Tears filled Ariane's eyes.

Renaldo said, "Gayle felt this was her punishment for not having taken better care of her father and then of me and Tony. She was always saying, 'This would have never happened if Mama had stayed.' That was how she saw it." He stood his elbows on his thighs and brought his palms together as if in prayer. Leaning his forehead against the arch of his hands he closed his eyes and wept.

Renaldo's descriptions of Gayle painted a canvas against which Ariane saw herself coming into view. She recalled

Gayle's words during one of her last sessions. *Mama was everything to me and Daddy. A part of him died with her. There was nothing I could do.* In her own warped way, Gayle had discussed these aspects of her life during sessions with Ariane.

Renaldo rubbed his eyes. "The cancer brought Gayle back to me, but for a short time." Gayle Clayton Baptiste had lived for six months after returning home to Renaldo and their son. "She refused to let me remarry her."

Ariane slid her hand into her pocket and touched the bracelet Jack had given her. She liked keeping it near, but felt it was too showy to wear—at least during the day.

"How's your son?" Questions about Gayle's daughter had simmered in Ariane since Gayle's death. Ariane gave a sad chuckle. "Gayle said you had a daughter." Another one of Gayle's lies to protect herself from what would have been Ariane's delving into her life had she known the full facts.

Renaldo smiled wryly. "He's tough—like Gayle, perhaps even stronger. Definitely stronger than me." Renaldo shook his head. "He was with her when she died."

She had been pained that Renaldo had denied her time with Gayle, but Ariane was overjoyed that he had permitted their son to experience what Ariane's aunt and uncle had denied her.

"I'd left the room." Renaldo's words pierced Ariane's joy.

"Fell apart when it became clear Gayle wasn't going to make it. I kept holding out hope." His lips began to tremble again. "I'd just returned with a cup of coffee. There she was holding Tony's hand. She was telling him how to take care of me."

Ariane's mother would not have needed to do that for her. Ariane's father had already died.

"She said, 'I love you and your father—both of you. Don't forget that.'" Renaldo sighed. "Life's circumstances had brought her back. Death was taking her away again."

"I tried to stay, but she was dying and there was nothing

I could do—this woman that I loved more than my parents, or sisters, anyone. I couldn't stand there and watch her die."

For Ariane, there was something about watching a person pass from this life to the next. All present were transformed. She had watched many people die. Renaldo had missed his wife's transition. Ariane wondered what she would have said to her mother and more importantly, to Gayle, had she been present.

Ariane had turned forty-two on July 5, the day after Gayle Clayton's death.

⁂

Three weeks had passed—the longest her mother had been in the hospital—when the little girl mixed into the crowd of adults in the lobby, and entered the elevator unnoticed by the guard. Three flights up, she emerged and went to her mother's room—number 206. The door was closed.

Foregoing a knock, she pushed it open and saw the bed, empty. Everything was gone—the flowers from the church, even the cards Ariane had made and sent each day to her mother by way of her aunt and uncle—her mother's elder brother.

Ariane's aunt had said, "She looks forward to your drawings. And those nice sayings—they give her joy." She had smiled and continued chopping carrots for the Sunday stew. "You keep on doing that—rest assured she's got all of them hanging on her wall." Her aunt's words made no sense in hospital room 206, which was absent of both her mother and the cards. Ariane had written the number on the envelope of every one sent.

Ariane gaped at the bed, which was stripped of linen. "May I help you?" Ariane turned around, startled.

"I came to see my momma." The nurse's eyes went still.

"The Grosvenors are your aunt and uncle?" The nurse collected herself once more. "I'll bet you're Ariane."

"Yes." Ariane nodded at the woman in white.

"They've talked of you often. And your cards..."

"I'm not supposed to be here, but I miss her—I need to see her." Again she scanned the empty walls, then stared to the bed in confusion. Perhaps her mother had left so they could clean the room. But where were the cards?

The nurse placed her arm around Ariane's shoulder, and moved to walk her from the room. Ariane slipped from her grasp. "Where is she? Where have you taken her?"

"Let's go call your aunt and uncle." The nurse tried approaching her.

"I want her back!" Ariane stomped her foot. "Take me to her now! Give me my momma back!" She kicked the nurse.

The nurse backed away, her lips trembling. Young and inexperienced, she said, "She died this morning."

⁂

During her first session, Gayle had turned the tables on Ariane. "Are you married?" The attorney was asking her therapist what Ariane normally asked her clients.

"Yes."

"How long?"

"Twelve years." Ariane didn't mention the request she had made to Jack the previous evening.

"I've done a lot of things to my husband and daughter I regret." Gayle added, "But I'm not going to talk about that." She changed the subject, and discussed her mother for a while. "She died of breast cancer. I was ten. I never said good-bye."

Ariane gave Gayle space to talk. "It's like this piece of you is missing." Gayle shook her head. "I work hard, win cases, try to be the best wife and mother, and there's no one to share in my glory, to feel proud of what I've done."

Ariane asked Gayle about her husband. "He's loving, an excellent father to our daughter," Gayle responded. Beyond that, Gayle's husband, Tony Clayton, was clearly not up for discussion. And Ariane didn't press the issue. She needed to keep working with Gayle. In some ways, she saw herself in Gayle.

She returned home that afternoon and told Jack, who was bewildered by her request for the divorce, that she no longer wanted it. Since he loved her so much, Jack accepted her change of mind, all the while wondering what had changed her mind, and what could alter it again.

⚜

Ariane would be seeing Renaldo as a client on a regular basis. "Gayle's sessions with you gave her the strength to be with Tony until the end, to say goodbye, to him."

Renaldo had dipped his head. "I'd like to keep seeing you, if possible."

Ariane hadn't planned on it occurring this way. But then she hadn't anticipated working with Gayle not once, but twice.

I've been running all my life. Death is telling me I need to live. Ariane remembered Gayle's words as she entered her bedroom and walked directly to the mirror. She raised her hand to touch it. "Hello," she said softly, and then, "Goodbye." She traced Gayle's reflection as it dissipated.

Ariane pulled the bracelet from her pocket and placed it on her wrist. The songs her mother had taught her to play filled her head. She went to the piano downstairs, and played each and every one.

Myrandha

Trey Williamson drew closer to his aunt, Mildred, who lay upon the hospital bed. She raised her head of matted, white hair, as if she wanted to get up.

"Lay back. You need to rest." Trey stroked her forehead. She had suffered a stroke three days earlier. The doctors said it was a miracle she hadn't died on the spot.

Mildred's brown eyes shone with urgency. " Your father—" she said in a raspy voice. "Promise me you'll talk to him."

Trey held Mildred's hand. He hadn't seen Skip Williamson in twenty-seven years—not since the funeral of Mildred's sister, Anne. Anne was Trey's mother and Skip's wife.

"You need to see him." Mildred's eyes entreated. "I need for you to do it, Trey. Promise."

Trey shook his head. Mildred fell asleep. Hours later she lapsed into a coma. She died the following day.

⁂

Trey steered his convertible from the garage beneath the building he had designed, and at which he now worked. He threaded his way to the San Francisco Bay Bridge and considered the promise Mildred had wanted him to make. He hadn't contacted Skip.

The morning after his mother's funeral, Trey awoke to an empty house. On entering his parents' room, he found their bed not slept in. Three envelopes containing letters stood on the bedside table. Skip had written them. The smallest and last one bore Trey's name.

"Go to Mildred and Avron's. Mildred will know what to do. Avron will explain." This was the extent of Skip's letter to Trey.

An obedient child, Trey did as Skip had instructed. Reaching Mildred and Avron's home, three doors down, he handed Mildred the letters. She took him into her arms and held him closer than his mother had. It was as if Mildred had been expecting Trey—had known what the letters contained.

Avron invited Trey into his study. "Your father's gone, Trey. You did nothing wrong. It's just the way Skip is." Avron pretended to look at the books lining the shelf against the wall. "Death affects people in many ways. Some never get over it."

"But Daddy loves me." Trey had felt a kinship with Skip, who was a private man—even beyond a standard father-son relationship. He had also developed a bond with Avron, one of guidance and love that could have developed into something deeper but for the restraint that came from both Trey and Avron, nephew and uncle. Trey never expected Avron to treat him as a son.

"Skip loves you. But we do too," Avron hugged Trey, something Skip had never done.

Skip's hobby was to shoot pictures on the weekend when he wasn't delivering mail. Trey would stand beside his mother or sit in her lap, her long, soft arms around him, with Skip snapping pictures from the distance. Skip later developed the photos in the darkroom he had built in the back yard.

Anne and Mildred had loved Skip's photography. Avron, more pragmatic, would tally accounts whenever he was away from the sales counter. He viewed Skip's photography as folly. At the time of Anne's death, Avron owned three stores in and around Baltimore. Skip, still working as a postman, could barely pay his mortgage.

Now three decades later, Trey had done well as an

architect with clients that kept him traveling the globe. Like Skip, life had made Trey a widower at a young age.

Trey was halfway across the Bay Bridge as he recalled Aunt Mildred's last words. *You need to go to Skip. Talk with him. He'll explain*—something she and Avron had not done.

Trey was weary of ruminating upon the knotted riddle binding him to his aunt, uncle, and father. He focused on the road. He was headed for his second blind date since Myrandha's death three years ago. The first one—six months ago—had been a disaster.

Trey had entered an easy conversation with his date, a calm, attractive woman. Then a voice rose from the table next to them. The female patron, sporting a short bob of pink hair, stood and began screaming at the man across the table from her. Trey's date fell still and silent. The pink-haired woman grabbed her steak knife, rushed around the table, and wrapping her arm around the man's neck, brought the blade to his throat.

Another woman appeared as if from nowhere. Strangely enough, she wore a lively pink dress almost matching that of the other woman's hair. A pearl choker circled her neck, highlighting the scooped neckline of her dress and the tensed line of her throat. A man, inches taller than her, stood to her back, a breath away from her braided hair..

Despite the drama unfolding before him, Trey's mind drifted to the many times he had inhaled the scent of Myrandha's hair, brushed aside her locks and kissed her neck…

Like Trey, who had loved Myrandha dearly, the man in the restaurant seemed more concerned for the woman in the pink dress than for the arguing couple. As if watching the scene from afar rather than the next table, Trey found himself wondering whether the man had given the woman the pearls she wore. Trey had chosen a similar strand for Myrandha on their fourth anniversary.

The woman in the pink dress spoke softly to the woman

holding the knife. "Don't do this, not to him, not to yourself." Her poise, tone, the tone of her words, had reminded Trey of Myrandha's manner when trying to make a point, particularly one he had not wanted to hear or understand.

After moments of hesitation with all in the restaurant seemingly afraid to breathe, the woman extended the knife past the man and to the palm of the woman wearing the pink dress. Tears of despondency filled her eyes as she moved to relinquish the weapon.

The knife came within a hairsbreadth of touching the palm of the woman in the pink dress. And then the near-victim spoke in a writhing, venomous tone. The violence that all observing had considered averted reared its angry head once more. The woman with pink hair snatched back the knife and set the blade to do its intended business.

The event had ended without bloodshed, but not without emotional consequences. When all was said and done, Trey drove his date home. He was a widower committed to remaining faithful to his wife's memory. This date marked his first attempt to explore the possibility of finding common ground with a woman for friendship and anything else that might emerge. Spellbound by the hostility that had erupted before them, he'd felt, instead, the effervescent spirit of Myrandha, and knew he wasn't ready to be with any other woman.

⁂

As Trey rolled off the Bay Bridge and exited onto Fremont Street, his cell phone rang. He hit the button to put it on speaker.

"Hey man, it's Mike. Hope you're on your way to the City. If not, it's my head. And two women will be doing the sawing."

"Calm down. I just cleared the bridge. I'm almost to Market Street."

"Whoa, you're early. You are committed to getting back into the swing of things. Or are you just trying to see this through?"

"I told you. I've got to get on with things." Trey had discussed the matter several times with Mike.

Trey made a right onto Market Street. The traffic light ahead flashed yellow then red. Trey slowed. The sun in his eyes, he lowered the visor. A picture of Myrandha fell onto his lap. Skip had taken the photo. Trey traced the edge of Myrandha's dark, smooth face. The light turned green, but he didn't notice until the car behind him honked impatiently. Trey jolted forward and made another right, this time onto Embarcadero.

"Are you there?" Mike called out through the speaker.

"Yeah, I'll see you in a few." Trey grabbed his phone and got out of the car, pulled up the hood of his jacket, and started toward the waterfront.

⁂

Trey had slept with his back to Myrandha the night before she left for Paris. Earlier that afternoon, he had discovered her with Skip at the kitchen table. She touched him several times in bed that night—her way of trying to get him to turn over and talk. He ignored her.

She kissed the back of his head the morning she was to leave. He got up hours later, removed the sheets from the bed, and threw them in the trash.

Promise me you'll find Skip. Please. Mildred's words had been Myrandha's wish too.

Mike summoned Trey again from the other end of the phone. "You know you don't have to go through with this. Kym and I can explain. Besides, Esther—"

"I'm here, Mike. Relax, I'll be there." Trey interrupted. He didn't hear his date's name. "It's 6:15." Their dinner was not until 7:00. "Just give me time."

Mike and Kym were friends of Trey and Myrandha. Mike had served as best man, Kym, maid of honor, at Trey and Myrandha's Las Vegas wedding. They had arranged Trey's first blind date six months earlier, and now this second one.

When Trey received Skip's panicked call saying that Myrandha might have been in the towers, Trey immediately called Mike in California. Thereafter, Mike spoke continuously with Skip, at first when Skip was still in Paris, and later as Trey and Mike worked to confirm whether or not Myrandha had been in the towers. Mike was there for Trey again when both he and Skip joined Trey in New York, as Trey dealt with the unbelievable.

Once in New York, Mike stood beside Trey as they listened to the Pakistani driver of the town car that met Myrandha at the airport. He explained that he had dropped her off at the World Trade Center about an hour before the disaster.

Like Mildred had during his mother's death, Mike and Kym saw Trey through Myrandha's.

Trey sat between Mike and Kym at memorial services for Myrandha in Las Vegas, her hometown. Mike watched as Skip approached Trey at the close of the ceremony. Skip tried speaking to Trey, but Trey walked away, hurt and angry that Skip had been the last person to see her. Mike later told Trey, "Skip's out there in limbo, man. And so are you. You need to invite him into your life, or tell him that a relationship won't work."

Since then, Mike saw a direct connection between Trey's avoidance of dating—moving forward with his life—and Trey's unresolved relationship with Skip.

Now walking down the Embarcadero, Trey turned back and peered up the Bay Bridge over which he had entered the City. *How many times did we drive across that bridge together?* Trey had first glimpsed Myrandha eight years ago. He had emerged from a building in Seattle—one that he had designed and overseen construction for. Myrandha, a professional model, had been posing as a cameraman encircled her, snapping shots as if she was a deity. Trey's building, her temple, cast a grand shadow.

Myrandha

Trey was taken by Myrandha's dark skin and deeply set eyes, black as night. They married a year later.

Trey continued walking, and remembering. He was to have met some Japanese businessmen at eight a.m. with plans for a building he was designing for their Osaka firm. They had requested a meeting at their New York branch office in the World Trade Center. Myrandha had completed her Paris shoot one day early. Unbeknownst to Trey, she flew to New York to surprise him. He was usually early for everything. He had planned to be there by eight that morning, but his cab was caught in traffic. Myrandha entered the North Tower at 7:45 a.m. At 8:46 a.m., Trey saw American Airlines Flight #11 slam into the tower. He didn't know Myrandha was inside.

⁙

Reaching Pier 39, Trey checked his watch and started back to MoMo's, site of the blind date. As he neared his convertible, his cell phone rang again. "I told you I'm here, Mike—"

"Trey, it's Skip. I hope it's not a bad time. I was just going through some—"

"Why are you calling?" The words slipped from Trey's lips. He instantly wished to reclaim them.

"Perhaps I should—I just—" Skip said.

Light from the dying late-August sun enveloped him, along with Myrandha's words. *He's your father.*

Skip cleared his throat and said, "How are you doing?"

Trey took the photo of Myrandha out of his breast pocket. He had carried it with him after it fell from the dash. He missed her smile. *Tell him how you feel,* Myrandha had often said. "It's been three years, and I still miss her."

"I know." Skip's words cautiously embraced Trey. "It was twenty-eight years ago today that I came home and found you holding your Momma." Trey had held Anne's lifeless head, cradled it while calling her name. "It's hard losing your wife," Skip said. "If you ever want to talk, you know I'm here."

The lump in Trey's throat softened. It had formed the day he entered his kitchen and found Skip talking with Myrandha. They'd been laughing.

"I'm over here in the City, just across from Pac Bell Park, Trey said. "Mike and Kym—they've set me up on this blind—"

"Come on over," Skip said. "It'll be good to see you." Skip's studio was just around the corner. Trey had gone there several times since Myrandha's death, but faced with the possibility of receiving the long-awaited answer to his question of why Skip had left, he had never gone inside. Trey wrote down the address, never letting on that he had come so close. He called Mike to say he would be late, and why.

***

Trey had surmised that the angry couple at the next table were man and wife. Kym's friend, Trey's date, sitting across from him, had seemed oblivious. Trey thought the look in the man's eyes said everything. The couple was married and had come to the restaurant to talk about a problem better discussed at home. Myrandha had pulled the same stunt on Trey concerning Skip.

She had just returned from a shoot in Bali. Trey had missed her terribly. He was also anxious to start a family, but Myrandha loved her work.

Avron had said it was best to let women make these decisions in their own time. "They're the ones who carry the babies. Mess up those first nine months for them, and you'll spend the rest of your life paying for it." His dark eyes always turned sad and wistful when he coached Trey on how to treat women. His advice had served Trey well with Myrandha until that night.

She smiled in a coy way that drew Trey to her. "There's something I have to tell you. Before I give you the good news, I want to tell you that I've met someone."

"Who?"

"Your father."

Trey's wine glass stopped in midair. "Don't play with me."

"He wants to talk with you." Myrandha's eyes held the look and hope of real possibility.

Soon after they met, Trey had explained to her how Skip had left the day after Anne's funeral. Myrandha had made it her goal to locate Trey's father. "You won't be happy until you know why he left," she coaxed. Trey feared Myrandha would not give him a child without meeting his father.

"How did you find him?" Trey asked coolly.

"*He* found me. Skip's my new photographer."

Trey stared at the roasted trout and asparagus on his plate. He had gone to considerable effort to prevent Skip from barging back into his life. Skip had tried contacting Trey when he graduated from architecture school, and later when Avron died.

"You can't work with him. I won't have it."

"But he's my photographer."

"I don't give a hoot what he is; I won't have you near that man."

"*That man* is your father." Myrandha's voice had been plaintive, betraying a deep yearning not just to assist in healing the estrangement between father and son, but also of uncovering something inside of herself. It was as if Myrandha not only wanted, but needed, to have Skip as her photographer, that some kind of bond had emerged between father-in-law and daughter-in-law, a connection that Trey could only touch or understand by reconnecting with Skip.

Trey stood and leaned close to Myrandha's ear. "You don't know the half of what you've done." He then spoke to the maître d', with whom he was well-acquainted, assured him that the service was wonderful, paid the bill, and went to the car.

When Myrandha didn't come, he went back inside. "She left through the back door," the maître d' explained. "He was an older man."

Skip! Trey's mind fired. He tried Myrandha's cell phone. Receiving no answer, Trey drove home to a dark and empty house.

The next day, he went to work, angry and hurt. Arriving home that afternoon, he had discovered Skip sitting at the kitchen table, talking with Myrandha.

"You have to leave," he said. He hadn't seen Skip in nearly three decades.

"He came to see *you*." Myrandha walked over to Trey. He stared past her at Skip's brown eyes, which verged on gray. His salt-and-pepper goatee matched the description given by the maître d'.

The words Skip had written in the letter to Trey had been seared onto his consciousness: *Avron and Mildred understand. Your Uncle Avron will explain.* Neither had, and Trey wasn't in the mood to hear it from Skip. He turned toward Myrandha's soft, ebony face, shocked at her betrayal. "Don't make him leave," she said, taking his arm.

Trey heard nothing as he shook her off and escorted a silent and withdrawn Skip to the door.

"How many times have you said you just wanted to know why he left?" Myrandha glared at the closed door, then Trey. "Now with the chance, you throw him out. He loves you, Trey."

"And where the hell were you last night?"

"In a hotel room. Skip took me there. You need to talk with him. How many times do I have to tell you things are not what they seem?"

The image of Myrandha sitting close to Skip at the table flashed across Trey's mind. The two had been smiling, Skip holding Myrandha's hand. "I know what I saw when I came in here this afternoon."

The room swirled around Trey. He recalled Avron's words: *Your mother's dead, Trey. Skip is gone. But you have us—your Aunt Mildred and me. I'm your father now.* Trey had never been certain of Avron's meaning: *I'm your father now.*

He gripped the banister and started upstairs.

Myrandha rushed to him. "Did you know that Skip helped you get into architecture school?"

Trey turned back. His face began to burn with the realization that this had not been Skip's first visit to their home. "How long have you known him?"

"You haven't answered my question," Myrandha said.

"How long have you known that man was Skip?"

Myrandha countered. "How do you think you got that scholarship? Your designs are great. But there were other talented students competing for that same scholarship. Skip had a client. He was on the board at USC. That client lobbied for you. He gave Skip monthly reports on how you were doing. I've talked with that man. He thinks highly of your father."

"Well, I'm glad someone does." He avoided Myrandha's eyes as he stormed out of the room. In their bedroom, he lay down upon the sheets Myrandha had placed on their mattress. He stared at the ceiling for what seemed like hours.

Myrandha kissed the back of Trey's head as he lay in bed the next morning with his eyes closed. She left the room, closed the door, and left for Paris, where Skip would be doing the shoot.

Skip called the afternoon of September 11. He had grown worried after hearing of the disaster and getting no reply from Myrandha's cell phone. "She went there to meet you and apologize," he told Trey.

He called Trey again, three weeks after the memorial service when Trey had refused to speak with him. Trey answered the telephone on the second ring. "Hello, son." Trey had been sitting at the desk in his office at Jack London Square, staring at Myrandha's picture. "Did you get the picture I sent?"

Trey moved to hang up, but Skip's voice came through once more: "I'm sorry for leaving you."

The image of Myrandha came in and out of focus. Trey zoomed in on her eyes, which were beckoning him to listen. He did not remember saying good-bye, and knew only that the two had understood each other without speaking.

That evening, as she had every night, Myrandha came to Trey in his dreams. He reached out to touch her, but she backed away.

Three years later, when Mike asked him to go on a second blind date, Trey searched Myrandha's face in the picture—and agreed to go.

Myrandha spoke to him in his dreams that night, her soft lips forming the words, *Forgive your father. I forgive you.*

He awoke to the darkness, and flicked on the bedside lamp. The picture of Myrandha was gone. Frantic, he got out of bed and searched around the nightstand, pulled apart the bedding. The picture fell from the covers. He picked up the black and white glossy Skip had sent, then lay back down clutching the picture, determined to try again to move forward.

Trey removed that same photo from his breast pocket and again marveled at Skip's ability to capture Myrandha's passionate soul. Though he was well-known for shooting pictures of the buildings he had designed, Trey did not photograph people. He now stood facing Skip's front door.

Skip ushered Trey into the loft with its fifteen-foot ceilings, and surveyed walls displaying black and white glossies of the faces and bodies Skip had photographed over the years. "You've come a long way," Trey said.

"So have we all." Skip closed the door and crossed to the window, which framed the Golden Gate Bridge. The wall of windows on the other side of the loft revealed the Bay and San Mateo Bridges.

"This is a nice place." Trey turned to the wall facing the door. A purple drape hung on it, covering what seemed to be a picture, eight or ten feet high. But for that, the wall was empty.

Skip handed Trey a glass of water. "I'm glad you came by."

Trey sipped. "This is nice crystal. Where'd you get it?"

"Client of mine gave it to me."

"The client who pushed for me to get the scholarship?"

Skip flinched at the underlying bitterness of Trey's words. "As a matter of fact, it was Myrandha. She gave them to me when I moved in here—a housewarming gift. Myrandha was a good woman."

"She came here?"

"Often." Skip pocketed his hands. For a moment Trey saw Myrandha's dark eyes looming within Skip's, brown mixed with gray, and longing for connection. He tightened his palm about the glass and stared at the purple drape.

Talk to him. He's your father. Myrandha's words slid along his thoughts. He sat his glass on the table to his left.

Skip's eyes glistened with tears. "You know, your mother was also a good woman. Don't ever forget that."

Trey checked his watch. "My dinner's at seven. I told them I'd be late, but seeing that it's fifteen past..." He stood.

Skip walked toward him. Skip had left messages over the last three years since Myrandha died—Trey's birthdays, Anne's, and then on what would have been Myrandha's thirty-fifth. "I took a lot from you when I left. I can never make up for that. But, I can at least—"

"Is that what Myrandha told you to say?"

"As a matter of fact, yes." Skip paused, struggling for the right words. "I know that Myrandha was pregnant when she died, son," he said.

Trey knew it too. On rising after Myrandha had left for Paris, he had torn the sheets from the bed. On his way to place them in the trash, the letter had fallen from their folds. Myrandha had written that Paris would be her last shoot—before settling down to raise their son. She was three months' pregnant.

Trey's chest grew tight.

"She told me on the shoot in Paris, just minutes before

she left for New York." Skip then said, "We have a lot in common, you and me," Each had been the last to see the other's wife before they died. Trey recalled Anne's last words: *Tell Skip I'm sorry.*

Skip contemplated the purple draping as he said, "That's what Myrandha wanted me to tell you, that she was sorry. I told her it would sound better coming from her."

Trey stiffened his jaw. Through the particles falling amid early-evening rays of sunlight, he pointed to the purple covering. Skip ran his fingers along the edges of the silk shroud. "It's made from a photo I took of Myrandha during the shoot in Paris." He pulled the ends of the drape. The sun's dying light cast a glow across the room.

Skip removed the drape. There, on the wall, hung an eight-by-ten-foot black-and-white photograph of Myrandha and Anne embracing. It was beautiful.

Trey felt a strange pull from behind. He turned back. A gold-framed snapshot of his mother stood on a small table against the opposite wall. Anne was holding Trey in her lap, his head resting on her chest. He was smiling.

Trey closed his eyes and inhaled the remembered scent of white lily talcum powder. His mother always wore it during the hot months of summer. She had been wearing it the day she died.

Skip said, "My success has carried the burden that it took your mother's death for me to realize my dream." Joy mixed with grief rose in Skip's eyes. The same brew of emotions had glimmered whenever he was about to snap a picture of Trey and Anne. "I lost everything that day."

Trey sighed deep into the irony of it all.

Talk to your father—before it's too late. Mildred's admonition rang in his mind.

Trey turned back to Skip. "Why did you leave me? Mildred and Avron never explained."

Skip's gaze wandered past him to the picture of Anne holding Trey.

"You were my *father*. Why?"

A glassy film slipped over Skip's eyes. "I'm not your father."

"What the hell do you mean?"

"I was your mother's husband, but I never legally adopted you. When your mother died, Avron—"

"Uncle Avron? What's he got to do with this?" Anger fed by misunderstood memories and lies filled Trey's chest.

"Your mother was pregnant with you when I met and married her. Avron was your father." Trey slumped onto the sofa. "I was her husband," Skip clarified. "Your birth certificate lists only Anne as your mother." Skip's words took on a monotone quality, like the shock-ridden drone of a new reporter reacting to images of the World Trade Center disaster. "Hospital records state Avron was your father. Anne also listed in her will that Avron was your real father."

Why would she do that? Trey massaged his temples.

For Trey, there was the act of terror that had taken Myrandha's life, and then there was Trey's own terror in having lost the third woman in his life whom he had loved. If only he could have said he was sorry for the way they had parted. Myrandha had come to the towers to do just that.

Skip's voice weakened. "I had no money. Avron owned the mortgage on the house we lived in. He could give you a better life. It was bad enough I had to let you go. I never imagined it would come to this."

Trey turned to the photograph of Anne holding him, then shifted his attention to the tall glossy black-and-white of her and Myrandha, standing arm in arm.

Mildred's words retraced their path. *Forgive me. Forgive Avron. We loved you. But Skip loved you like a father.*

⁂

Trey entered MoMo's, a different restaurant from where he had taken his first date, and also from the one in which he and Myrandha had quarreled. No bad memories here.

Seeing Trey, Mike hurried over to meet him. With a look

of bewilderment on his face, Trey immediately described the huge picture of Anne and Myrandha. "It was beautiful, astonishing. He really knows what he's doing." Trey then told Mike what he had learned from Skip. "I don't know who I am or who to trust."

Avron and I loved you. But Skip loved you like a father's supposed to.

Mike laid his hand upon Trey's back. Tears glistened in Trey's eyes. "He gave me back Myrandha—and Momma. But I don't know if I want him."

After Mildred's death, Trey had confided in Mike as to why that first blind date had gone awry, of how the violent restaurant scene had affected him. "It was as if Myrandha was right there, watching me." He then told of Mildred's request that he contact Skip. "It was Myrandha's wish too."

"Skip's your father, Trey."

Trey followed Mike to their table. Drawing near, he stopped when he recognized the woman sitting next to Kym.

Esther. She had been Trey's first blind date.

Mike patted Trey's shoulder.

Trey extended his hand to Esther and attempted to apologize for not having returned her call after their date.

"Don't worry about it." Esther shook her head. "My husband died in a car accident last year. The restaurant incident left me shaken too. My husband and I went there a lot. There's no way you could have known."

"Like I said," Mike said to ease the awkward moment. "Everyone's struggling."

Esther squeezed Trey's hand again and sat down. The air seemed to vibrate for a moment and his vision blurred. Then slowly, inexplicably, Esther transformed into Myrandha. "I forgive you," Myrandha said, but only Trey could hear her. The sound of her voice rippled through his chest. His mind struggled to understand how and why Myrandha was sitting before him, as Esther. She stood, separating herself from Esther, then moved behind Esther's chair.

Anne materialized beside Myrandha. Both were as they had been in Skip's photograph, wearing billowy white gowns. Their smiles bequeathed to Trey the physical and eternal joy both had possessed in life and in death.

"She's nice, Trey." Myrandha pointed to the back of Esther's head. Anne nodded in agreement. Myrandha's demeanor, though loving and compassionate, seemed different from the night she told him of Skip's serendipitous entrance into her life, of them having developed a bond that needed Trey's approval, his seal of love and forgiveness.

During the height of the violent incident in the restaurant where he had attempted his first date, the woman in the pink dress had spoken with the same comfort and concern expressed by Myrandha's spirit. Anne and Myrandha smiled at Trey, and as his vision faded, Myrandha blew him a kiss.

He wanted to follow them. Instead he closed his eyes.

What to him had been time immeasurable, had been but a moment to his dinner companions. Trey opened his eyes, extended his hand to Esther a second time, and added, in the formal way Anne had taught him, "Forgive me for arriving late." His heart was brimming with sadness and joy as he added, "My father called."

In Baghdad

Captain Daryl Sharpton made a three-hundred-and-sixty-degree turn, and again surveyed the room, empty of chairs, sofa, curtains, and family pictures. The bedroom closets upstairs were empty. Only his hat and dress greens—evidence of life before Baghdad, Iraq—remained. Gone also were Sharpton's wife Lisa and their sons. Daryl suspected they might be at her aunt's home in Oakland, California. That was three days' drive from Redstone Arsenal in Alabama, where he had been stationed for the last five years.

Daryl, who was to have retired in March 2003, withdrew his discharge papers and reenlisted after the invasion of Iraq. He wanted to accompany his men to Baghdad. Lisa had begged him not to go, and Daryl had considered for a moment Lisa's warning, "This is not your war."

But Daryl had served in the Persian Gulf, and wanted to protect his men. "They're barely boys, Lisa. It's fierce over there."

"Like life isn't fierce here?" Lisa's brown eyes had shone with fury. Daryl had also served in Desert Storm.

Unlike most captains, he remained loyal to the privates and corporals barely weaned from their mothers' breasts and serving under him. Daryl Sharpton had earned his rank on and off the battlefield. His decision to return to the Middle East had been one of duty and conscience.

"They need someone to watch over them," Daryl pled his case. "Someone who cares for them, someone who knows what they've been through. Nobody cares for black men."

"And you think you're the one to do it?"

"Why not me? Who better?" Daryl's grandfather had been a private in World War II after African Americans won the war at home to defend their country abroad. Daryl's father, a drill sergeant, served in both Korea and Vietnam. Both men had given their best. Each had instilled in Daryl a sense of loyalty toward those who served under him—a quality not displayed by most senior officers.

Lisa stepped closer and searched Daryl's eyes. "Have you considered that maybe, just maybe, you're not the best person to do that?"

"What do you mean?" Daryl's cheeks were burning.

"Haven't you been watching television? The Iraqis don't have slanted eyes, Daryl. They're not Vietnamese we can distinguish ourselves from, who act like what we're doing doesn't matter—that they don't count. This war is with people who look like *us*." Lisa dug deeper. "Or have you forgotten what happened over there in 1990?"

Daryl was running solo checks on his men patrolling the Kuwait-Iraq border near a small town close to the Tigris River in the Persian Gulf. A man stepped into the path of Daryl's jeep as he drove between checkpoints. Daryl swerved violently and missed the man. His jeep turned over, throwing Daryl onto the desert floor.

Daryl was alone, hot, and hungry, shaken from the rollover. The man held what appeared to be bread wrapped in cloth.

The man smiled, extended his hand as he neared Daryl. The cloth fell away and a gun emerged. Two shots sounded.

Daryl fired back. Once, twice, a third. And then a fourth. He scrambled to his feet, and the other man lay unmoving. Gun still drawn, Daryl cautiously approached—and looked down upon a dead man. The smile was still on his face.

Aside from the turban and dress, the man resembled Daryl's Uncle Wayne.

Daryl had pushed the incident into the crevices of his conscience. He had told no one what he had done, or what had nearly occurred until he arrived home in 1992.

"I almost got tripped up," he said, when explaining to Lisa how he was nearly killed.

"What happened?" She asked, in horror of what could have been, a story she might have never heard.

"I was lonely." Daryl said, bemused. "I wanted to be with someone … hungry … he looked like *me*."

"You said he reminded you of your Uncle Wayne?"

"He did … after he was dead. But when I was standing over him … "

⁕

Daryl's mind sank back to why he was now home, in an empty house, no longer enlisted in his country's war. *Why did he do it?* He was subsumed by the emptiness resulting from his actions in Baghdad.

Daryl's Uncle Wayne had never served in a war. He was a pacifist who had supported Martin Luther King Jr.'s efforts to end the war in Vietnam and bring American troops home.

Daryl's mother badly wanted Daryl's father home, yet she criticized her brother Wayne's efforts. The rift between sister and brother grew wide. They stopped speaking after Dr. King's death in April of 1968. Daryl, then eight, didn't hear from Wayne until two mornings after his thirty-second birthday, when he was leaving for the Persian Gulf.

Daryl's mother delivered Wayne's letter, tucked in an envelope with peace signs from the sixties. The two lines read: *Don't go. This is not your war.*

Thinking his uncle's words ludicrous, Daryl laid the note on the bureau and joined his men on the flight field that afternoon. Two years later, Daryl recalled his uncle's warning.

Lisa had presented Daryl with the letter when he explained how he was nearly killed. She repeated those words over a decade later, when Daryl, then a captain, reenlisted to accompany his men to Iraq. *Don't go. This is not your war.*

Those words rang in his head again in August 2003. A mortar had exploded in their encampment outside of Baghdad and sent Daryl to the ground. He opened his eyes to the reality of what he had done: Private Johnson was lying next to him, the top half of his skull gone. His lifeless eyes betrayed Daryl's error. Captain Daryl Sharpton had shot one of his own men before the blast.

Daryl hoisted the nineteen-year-old body into his arms and screamed into the fiery madness, "Why did you put on this fucking turban?"

Johnson had gone missing three weeks earlier while on a routine mission scouting the ten-mile perimeter surrounding Daryl's encampment. Daryl declared him captured after five days, fearing that he had been killed—or worse, beaten and tortured.

Johnson had broken free from enemy captors and stormed the camp ahead of them. Unrecognizable in the turban, he created a stir, alerting Captain Sharpton's sergeant that guerillas were headed their way.

The small band of guerrillas behind Johnson leveled mortars and grenades before the majority arrived. The few minutes between Johnson's arrival and his captors' invasion of the encampment gave Sharpton's infantry time to arm themselves.

Angry, and repulsed by the horror of the bombs exploding around him, Daryl fired as much out of a sense of failure as of saving his life. Fifteen of Sharpton's one hundred men sustained wounds. Johnson, on his way to Captain Sharpton, was the only one killed. Immediately after he shot Johnson, the mortar knocked Sharpton down.

⁂

Sharpton surveyed his living room once more. He had stood there when Lisa begged him not to go. "It's time to stop. Let someone else fight."

"But this is all I know." Daryl drew her close.

"Then learn something else." Daryl laid his head upon her shoulder and ached inside. He needed to learn something else ... Now, carrying the burden of his greatest crime, the vacancy and spiritual impotence resulting from his actions in Baghdad devoured him once more. Was it too late to redefine his life? And what of the value of his life? Why had the forces of the universe kept him alive and rendered the man back in Kuwait, and then Private Johnson, unto death? Daryl put on his hat and left his empty house behind.

⚜

The face of the man in the doorway told Daryl all he needed to know. Chauncey Holmes, the judge advocate general and Daryl's friend, knew where Lisa had gone. "Have a seat," he said somberly. "When did you get back?"

"Just now."

"Have you checked the mail?" Chauncey spread his elbows along the edge of his desk. Like Daryl, he wore dress greens.

"Should I? The house speaks for itself." Or rather, its emptiness did. "Did you know about Lisa going away?"

"She had wanted to leave the furniture, but—" Daryl stood and headed for the door. Chauncey overtook him, and held the door closed. "I heard what happened over in Iraq—I couldn't get to Lisa in time."

"In time? Do you really think that mattered? She's obviously been planning this."

"Lower your voice." Chauncey matched Daryl's frustrated tone. "It's not what you think."

"And just what is it? I come home after killing one of my men and find my fucking house empty, my boys gone, and not a word from my wife as to where she's taken them. What am I supposed think? No, you just tell me what I am not getting right here, Chauncey." Daryl's ears felt as if they were on fire.

"It is what you see, but there's more."

Daryl crossed his arms. "Let me guess. Lisa's bought a house somewhere close, and you're supposed to take me to where she's waiting with a surprise party of people to welcome me home."

"You're not the only one who went to war. Lisa's had enough." Daryl didn't like the ominous ring in Chauncey's voice. "Others with less than you have returned from Iraq to find their homes empty. At least you can walk and see."

Daryl bit the inside of his cheek. If only he didn't see Johnson's face. It was forever before him.

"Do you know where she is?"

Chauncey gave a long sigh. He had served with Daryl, both first lieutenants in the Persian Gulf. On returning, he went to law school and returned to full service as a judge advocate general. In the last year of the war with Iraq, he had overseen hundreds of divorces, some with the enlisted persons present, and others done over the wire. Chauncey had urged Daryl to reconsider going to Iraq.

Daryl reached for the doorknob. Chauncey grabbed his arm. "She's tired. Give her some time." Lisa Sharpton had endured twenty-six years of not knowing Daryl's location or the level of hostility where he was. As Daryl was head of a special operations unit until last year, his work was classified. "Don't go and do something foolish," Chauncey said.

"Considering what I did in Iraq, my actions can only get better." Daryl again reached for the doorknob.

"Private Johnson enlisted after 9/11." Chauncey's tone was firm. "He knew what he had put in for. He wasn't Lisa, Todd, or Christian."

Chauncey handed Daryl a piece of paper. "She's in Oakland. But like this nation, she needs time to rethink and heal."

Daryl swallowed hard. Lisa had been the perfect soldier's wife, and like the man she married, she kept her fears close to her heart.

The thought of never laying beside her again was agonizing. Frantic from his ill-fated actions, Daryl had tried calling Lisa from his hospital bed during the days following the attack. He had wanted to say, "Sorry. You were right," then provide a better life for her and their sons. Due to repeated attacks, he hadn't gotten through.

Chauncey clasped Daryl's shoulder. "Beverly's gone to her mother's, and I've requested early retirement." Daryl forced himself to stand still as Chauncey, who had been shot in Kuwait, hobbled back around his desk. "We're not near a divorce, but…" Again Chauncey sighed, then half smiled. "Funny thing is, I think she could have survived me remaining enlisted. It's me who's losing it."

Daryl thanked Chauncey and left the office.

※

Tears had slid down Todd's eight-year-old face on the afternoon Daryl left for Iraq. Eleven-year-old Christian, like Daryl, was stoic. Lisa, having said her piece, folded her slender arms and turned away when Daryl hugged the boys.

A swell of vulnerability pulsed through Lisa's taut lips when Daryl kissed her. He almost turned around upon reaching his jeep. Had the driver not been awaiting Daryl's command…

But what was a Captain without a command, an army? All were lost and searching for leadership and protection from an enemy without and within.

Daryl's mother had stood by his father, Glenn Sharpton, through double tours in Vietnam. The drinking he brought home from Saigon stayed with him for life. He died in a VA hospital from cirrhosis of the liver, never having seen Daryl's sons.

"Stick close to your men," Glenn had ordered Daryl.

"Don't abandon 'em." *Follow them. And they'll follow you.* Daryl would never leave his men or his father.

It hadn't mattered that Daryl had graduated from college or gotten married. When Daryl told his father of Christian and Todd's births, his father had simply smiled, nodded, and asked, "How're your men?"

The army had been Glenn Sharpton's life, and it was Daryl's way of remaining close to his father. Shooting Private Johnson severed Daryl's connection with his father, and to himself. Daryl needed to remake himself into something beyond war and fighting. He had to get to Lisa and say, "I'm sorry."

A three-hour flight to California would leave no time to think. He headed for his car.

❋ Daryl drove down the freeway leading from downtown Oakland. Except for the houses perched in the hills, the Oakland landscape resembled what Daryl had left in Iraq. He had driven for three days and needed to decide between checking into a hotel and sleeping in his car again. Either way, he was alone.

He glanced at the slip of paper lying on the passenger's seat—he had kept it there the entire journey. Chauncey had written a name and number beside Aunt Hannah's home number: *Drew Clarke. 510-555-3534.*

"He's a friend of mine. Helped me get into law school. Corporate, but a good guy." Chauncey had torn the paper from his pad. "His father was in Vietnam. They're good people."

Daryl exited right, and started down San Pablo Avenue. The scenery seemed tranquil enough—pedestrians walking down the street on a clear afternoon, with the sun setting into the West.

Do these people know what's going on in the world? Daryl squeezed the steering wheel. He had lived his entire life in the East.

The intersection light flashed red as Daryl approached

the four-way stop. A church stood to his right, a temple of some sort on his left. The men entering the temple wore turbans, some red, others green, and still others blue. The women were garbed in colorful flowing saris. The faces of the men wearing turbans ranged in color from nearly white to dark brown. Many of the women in saris were white Americans.

What sort of place is this? he thought as he parked in a space in front of the temple. He felt like an orphan who'd done all the right things, but there was no one to take him home. He had not shaved or bathed in three days. His body itched. Daryl detested poor hygiene, and he hated himself.

A hand knocked on his window. He rolled it down to a young African American woman with freshly done dreads.

"Are you alright, sir?"

A civilian for the first time in over two decades, he tried not to sound as if he was giving orders. "I'm fine."

Her eyes registered the clutter of empty food wrappings from McDonald's, Burger King, and the like. "Have you eaten?" He lowered his head. "There's a festival inside the temple. We're serving a meal. It's vegetarian, but the ticket's only..." She pulled one from her purse and extended it through the window. "Here, take mine."

"No, let me pay for it. I have the money." Daryl reached for his pocket, but when he extended her the twenty, her smile weakened.

It seemed innocent, what he had fought to preserve in Iraq. This woman, part of his culture, looked like so many of the Iraqi women his men had left widowed. Private Johnson's wife, now a widow, had been expecting. *Why had Johnson worn that damn turban?* More men wearing turbans that hid their hair strode up the street and entered the temple. A wave of confusion swept over the former soldier.

The young woman, no more than twenty, still stood at the window saying, "Please. Everyone is welcome."

⁂

The food, though without meat, was good. Not too heavy. It filled Daryl and left room for him to think.

That night he entered one of the hostel rooms in the back of the temple at the *siddha* ashram. He lay down, still wearing his uniform. *What will I say to Lisa?* He fell asleep clutching the thought.

Daryl woke early the next morning, and showered for the first time since leaving Alabama. He dressed in his formal greens, put on his hat, and walked out of the temple.

Women in flowered hats and men in crisp suits entered the church perched on the corner diagonally across from the temple. It was Sunday. Lisa was probably in church with her Aunt Hannah.

Lisa's Aunt Hannah was nothing like Daryl's family. Carefree and yet levelheaded, she had been married for forty years and had raised three sons and two daughters. Hannah was nice to Daryl, yet some part of him was resistant toward getting to know her, letting her in. She frightened him.

A churchwoman who prayed fervently, Hannah's laissez-faire manner toward life disturbed Daryl. It was as if she had surrendered to some higher power forever revealing itself, and of which she had no intention of evangelizing. Hannah Martin concentrated on inner devotion and love for God by nurturing those around her. She searched for life's true meaning by living from within. Her husband, a former military man, seemed not to mind. Nor did she seek to bind him to her beliefs, if you could call them that. She had encouraged Lisa to meditate. "The wife of a military man has to know the worth of prayer. Without it she'll die." Her tender words had rung menacingly.

Daryl felt that his career had been an injustice, an imposition, on Lisa's life. Perhaps if he had chosen a noncombat-oriented role in the military, something less physical and dirty, then Hannah would not have spoken with such fervor. But then, Hannah's husband had been a Marine Captain.

What Daryl hadn't heard, that Hannah had also said, was, "Without prayer you'll die, Lisa, and so will Daryl—neither of you knowing why."

Hannah spoke to him in a dream as he slept that night in the ahsram's hostel. "Life without prayer leaves us open and unguarded." Daryl lay dying. Lisa and his Uncle Wayne stood over him, as he had done to the man in Kuwait.

You'll die—and neither of you will know why ...

.❧.

Daryl started toward the church across the street. Reaching the church doors, he peered in, then took a seat in the third pew from the back, on the right aisle. Lively organ music arose from the front of the church and signaled the start of the service. The choir entered the sanctuary triumphantly swaying to the soul-stirring rhythm.

A minister who appeared generations younger than Daryl followed. He shook the hands of parishioners seated next to the aisles. He took hold of Daryl's hand and smiled, saying, "Good to see you, brother," and proceeded up the aisle to the pulpit. The young minister's hand had felt warm and comforting. His eager expression reminded Daryl of Private Johnson. The minister began his message. "The Lord loveth those whom He chastiseth." Robed in black, he stood tall. His words hung in the air a moment before he continued. "This country—our country— is at war with itself and everyone else." Daryl's temples began to throb. "Most of us don't know who or what we're fighting—or even why. *Our* boys are dying." The minister pounded the lectern. "So are we."

Daryl jumped as the word *our* landed in the flat soil of his mind and overturned the loyalty that had informed his decision to return to war.

The minister then said, "A friend of mine who reads the *Qur'an* says that God instructs us, "No nation can outrun its term. Nor can they lag behind. The *Qur'an* also teaches that God made man from clay and black mud. Now I'm not a Muslim. Neither am I a scholar of the *Qur'an*." The young minister leaned back, his robe swaying. "But I know God loves us. He loves us all."

He took in breath, and with keen perception studied the audience. "The *Qur'an* also says that God is without attribute. God has no face. Perhaps when God is without a face, every face that comes before us is holy.

"My fellow brothers and sisters, I'm tired. I'm tired of the hate. The hate we have for others. The hate we have for ourselves.

"Christ commands us to love others as He loves us. Our Lord also invites all who are burdened and heavy-laden to Him, and He will give us rest." Again the young minister stood tall. He clapped his hands in motion with the organ music that again filled the church. The choir began singing.

As the minister urged those burdened to come forth, Daryl left a fifty-dollar bill in the collection plate, pushed open the doors of the sanctuary, and stepped outside. He had been baptized in the vestry pool at his church in Georgia and washed in the blood of Private Johnson.

Daryl paid for a week's stay at the hostel behind the ashram. He passed through the temple hall, empty of people but filled with the sweetness of sandalwood. The pounding of his heart slowed. His chest, tight and constricted for weeks, relaxed. Again he breathed in.

His uncle's words echoed within. *This war's not for you. You've done enough.* And then Lisa's plea. *Let someone else protect. I need you here. I'm afraid.* Daryl's fingers, numb from Lisa's absence, began to tingle.

The words sounded from behind him. "Everyone is holy." He turned around in time to see Lisa walk through the entrance of the ashram and enter the temple hall through the doors nearest the entrance. She was wearing a pink sari. The woman beside her wore a green one, green that matched her eyes.

Daryl entered the temple doors at his end of the hall. Lisa and the other woman had not seen him. They continued inside, sat on two cushions, and gazed up at the five-foot bronze statue of a six-armed god at the front of the temple. The deity was dancing in a ring of fire.

A black and white photo of a smiling woman covered the wall behind the icon. The woman was of color—most likely brown—like Lisa, and the woman with her, the woman with green eyes. Brown skin and brown eyes, like Private Johnson. And like Daryl.

Daryl fell to his knees and brought his palms together. Silence. He opened his eyes and slowly lifted his head. The temple was empty.

Another dream? Daryl got to his feet, bewildered and cross that he couldn't understand. He thought he had done everything right—had just now prayed, begged even.

The slip of paper bearing Lisa's name and that of Chauncey's friend fell to the floor. Daryl didn't remember having taken it with him to church. He picked it up and pulled out his cell phone on his way out of the temple.

Drew slid the sugar dish across the kitchen table to Daryl. He had offered Daryl green tea with a hint of jasmine.

"Have you considered what you're going to do now that you're retired?"

"No, I haven't." Daryl stared into his cup. He was accustomed to basic military rations.

"I'm not sure if Chauncey told you, but my father went to Vietnam." Drew sipped his tea. "It was hard on my mother. It was hard on me. It hurt my dad the most." Drew's brown eyes bore sadness. "Some say the war in Iraq is headed that way.

"I remember when my father came back from his second tour," Drew continued. "It's taken him the twenty years since retirement to recover. Some things he still can't discuss. We've grown closer in the past years." Drew

turned toward the kitchen window. "But it's still hard."
Daryl stood abruptly, despite his fear of being rude. "I need
to go." He was grateful that Chauncey had given him Drew's
number, but anxious about it too. Even with his herbal tea,
and though not a serviceman, Drew was easy to talk to. A
bit too easy, and Daryl still needed to find Lisa. He started
for the door.

"Let me walk you out." Drew escorted him through the
foyer toward the front door. "You'll need to come back. I'll
introduce you to my father. I'm sure you and he—"

A key sounded in the door leading up from the garage.
"Oh, that would be Raven, my wife." He glanced back. "She
went out with a friend, someone she just met." Drew did
not know Raven's friend, had not seen her. "If you have a
moment—" He let go of the handle and retraced his footsteps
across the foyer and to the garage door then opening.

Raven stepped inside. She was wearing a green sari, but
Daryl didn't notice. He was looking at the woman behind
Raven—the woman wearing pink. They were as Daryl had
seen them in the *siddha* temple.

"Raven, this is Captain Daryl Sharpton. He's a friend of
Chauncey's." Drew then turned to Daryl. "This is my wife,
Raven." He seemed unaware of the quagmire entrapping
him and Raven.

"And I'd like you both to meet my friend—"

"How did you know to come here?" Lisa said in a small
voice.

"I didn't. It was the dream..." Daryl's last word drifted
into overturned memories of his misdeeds, his confusion
and desperation. He lowered his head. "I needed to find
you..."

Lisa rushed past Raven and Drew standing to either
side of her and Daryl, placed her arms about Daryl's chest,
and kissed his lips. "It's alright," she said. "It's alright. I'm
here."

❋ While Daryl was in Iraq, the doctors had informed Lisa she had breast cancer. Emotionally reeling, and preoccupied with the practicalities of moving her family nearer to her Aunt Hannah for support, Lisa had left for Oakland days before the attack, unable to reach her husband. "I tried calling Baghdad, but they said you'd left."

Drew gracefully filled the silence that followed her words. "I bring clients here a lot," he said, indicating the restaurant where they were having dinner, one which he had told them held significant memories for him. He made eye contact with Raven, whose expression became apprehensive. "One night things fell terribly apart ... but that's a story for another day. We're here in honor of you." Like Drew, Raven had insisted that Daryl and Lisa's reunion needed celebration so they had driven the couple to the City.

Later Daryl and Lisa were alone at the table. Drew had gone across the room to speak with a colleague he'd spied earlier. He'd taken Raven with him. Against the hubbub of voices in the restaurant, Lisa slid her hand into Daryl's.

"I was so worried," she said in a broken voice. "I thought I'd lost you and that I would die from this." Having sat through the entire meal genial and composed, she now touched her breast and began to cry. Daryl's eyes softened with his own tears.

"I came to Aunt Hannah's so I could have some help with the boys. I also needed spiritual support. I met Raven the day before my first round of chemo. She knows Aunt Hannah from the ashram."

"I thought Hannah was Christian."

"She is, but she likes going to the ashram too. Their leader is a woman. Aunt Hannah likes what she has to say. She's a woman of color—brown like Hannah."

Brown like you and me, Daryl considered. He cleared his throat, squeezed Lisa's hand. "You were right, Lisa. I should've never gone." The image of Private Johnson's body riddled with bullets from Daryl's gun and shaking with death rose before Daryl. "I made a big mistake." His words, soft and aching, teemed with remorse.

"You did the best you could."

"You don't understand. I shot—"

"You killed Private Johnson."

Daryl leaned back in his chair, taken by surprise. "How did you know?"

"His wife wrote me. She had the baby—a little girl. She wanted you to know that it wasn't your fault." Lisa reached into her purse then and handed Daryl the letter.

At first I was hurt and angry. I wanted to kill myself for letting him go and then you for shooting Emmett. But Emmett kept coming to me—in my dreams. The night before I had the baby he explained: Cap'n didn't know who he was shootin'. He thought I was one of the enemies...

Daryl lifted his head. "I shot a black man—a man who looked like me. If Private Johnson had been white—" Lisa pulled Daryl into her arms. "This war is too close to home." He breathed in the scent of her, chamomile and sandalwood, light and dark—both of which had died while in the deserts of Iraq and Baghdad. Daryl then considered his country. America...how paradoxical and strange its ideologies, its people ever more confused. And in this he, too, was changing. "This war is too close to home," Daryl repeated.

"But you're home now. You're safe."

Cap'n didn't know who he was shootin'. He thought I was the enemy. Emmett Johnson's words ebbed and flowed from the letter and into Daryl's heart. Again he breathed in Lisa's scent, sandalwood and safety. He was home.

Acknowledgments

This book would not have been possible without my parents, Geneva and Johnnie Weeks; Bay Area writing teacher Clive Matson, who accepted my stories right from the start; fellow Goddard Alumna, Elaine Elinson, who assisted me in gaining the opportunity to "Come as you are; leave the way you want to be;" and my Goddard mothers, Mariana Romo-Carmona and Beatrix Gates, who taught me to believe in myself, and to read and write like an author.

Thank you a thousand times over to Edward Messner, MD, for demanding that I embrace and care for myself; to Charlotte Whitaker Lewis, PhD, who first introduced the idea that my depression was suppressed creativity; to Bruce Cribley, MFT, who allowed as much time in my sessions to discuss my stories as my role as a psychotherapist; and to Dr. Maria Chiaia, MFT, PhD, psychotherapist, and fellow Goddard alumna, who nurtured me through the process of becoming a psychotherapist, and developed my understanding of the human psyche. Many thanks to Marlin Griffith, PhD, for allowing me to see that psychotherapy is as much a search for healing as it is an act of facilitating healing in those with whom we work. The sincerest of gratitude to Gerald Davenport, PhD, for teaching me that healing is a choice we assert in every decision we make.

I offer praises and gratitude to Bishop Nelson Major Midgette, whose sermons took me many times to heaven and back.

To Dada Agra: I hold the fondest of memories of the meals you prepared and served me in Los Altos—the food of Siva, sustenance upon which I continue to thrive.

With the deepest of appreciation, I thank Sheik Yassir Chadley who, while striding up and down the side of Willard Pool, taught me to cut through the water and swim, not against, but with my fears, and that a Sufi is one who dwells between hope and fear.

To Father Leo Edgerly for all the late entrances I've made, when you stated I'd arrived "right on time, God's time." I repay you by exhibiting more patience and gratitude with myself and with others.

I thank my spiritual sisters, Naima and Joy, ever ready to hear my woes and support whatever my endeavors. I am certain we have known each other lifetimes.

To fellow author, Lisa G. Riley: thanks for all the times you've let me assist you in trying to make sense of the tangled dreams of writers. Speaking to you loosened my knots. For Phillip Wilhite and

Dera Williams, your sincerity as supportive scribes is invaluable. I'm looking forward to seeing your stories in print.

To my publisher and editors, Linda Meyer and Laura Meehan: you've allowed me a creative freedom in which I have had enormous fun and learned so much.

To Allison Collins and Liz Fuller: you're the absolute best marketer and publicist any writer can have.

Samantha, Meredyth, and Naomi: My love for you can never match your enduring patience with me as I strive to become all of what I hope for you.

Jon, as always, "I love you."

Bis millah ir rahman ir rahim. May God's peace reign upon any and every person who encounters this book, and whose eyes search the dunes of these pages.
—Anjuelle Floyd

Three Muses Press thanks the following people for their work on
Keeper of Secrets ... Translations of an Incident

❖ Editing ❖
Laura B. G. Meehan, Katrina Hill

❖ Design ❖
Laura Dewing

❖ Marketing ❖
Allison Collins, Elizabeth Fuller, Erin Malus, Cassie Richoux

Special thanks to Mary Ann Schelb for her box of secrets.

—Linda M. Meyer, publisher
Three Muses Press

Three Muses Press is an imprint of Ink & Paper Group, LLC
David Cowsert, CEO
Linda M. Meyer, COO, Editor in Chief
Cameron Marschall, CFO, CIO
Allison Collins, VP of Marketing & Sales
Bo Björn Johnson, Chairman of the Board

and let's not forget
Jennifer Weaver-Neist, Manager of Miscellaneous Wonders
Selah Meehan, The Real Boss